Praise for the British edition of *Edge of Nowhere*

". . . a stark and profound tale.... A powerful novella that grips you tight and doesn't let go." —*The Bookseller*

"A great story; a nail-biting tale of triumph." —*The Bookbag*

"A hard-edged adventure story." —*The Guardian*

"A book ready to challenge the supposed superiority of *Robinson Crusoe* in the adventure genre, boasting considerably more psychological edge and an equally thrilling storyline." —*Radiowaves*

"A tale of triumph over adversity, a boy's determination to survive and a father who never gives up hope. A powerful and exciting novel." —*The Harbour Bookstore*

National Literary Trust's 2010 National Young Reader's Recommended Booklist Selected Book, Young Teen Fiction Award (UK)

Short-listed for the 2011 Hull Award for Children's Literature (UK)

Books by John Smelcer

Fiction

Lone Wolves
The Trap
The Great Death
Alaskan: Stories from the Great Land

Native Studies

The Raven and the Totem
A Cycle of Myths
In the Shadows of Mountains
Trickster
The Day That Cries Forever
Durable Breath
Native American Classics
We are the Land, We are the Sea

Poetry

The Indian Prophet
Songs from an Outcast
Riversong
Without Reservation
Beautiful Words
Tracks
Raven Speaks
Changing Seasons

EDGE *of* NOWHERE

John Smelcer

Leapfrog Press
Fredonia, New York

Published in 2014 in the United States by
Leapfrog Press LLC
PO Box 505
Fredonia, NY 14063
www.leapfrogpress.com

First published in 2010 by Andersen Press Limited
London UK

Printed in the United States of America

Distributed in the United States by
Consortium Book Sales and Distribution
St. Paul, Minnesota 55114
www.cbsd.com

First Edition

ISBN: 978-1-935248-57-6

Library of Congress Cataloging-in-Publication Data

Information is available from the Library of Congress.

for Zara, who never once disappointed me

Acknowledgements

The author would like to thank his editor, Bard Young, as well as Rod Clark, Sue Romanczuk, David Collins, Elizabeth Maude, Eloise King, Jack Vernon, Lisa Graziano, Dan Johnson, and Katy Kortie. A belated thanks go to John Updike and Frank McCourt for their helpful editorial advice.

Alutiiq words are from the author's *The Alutiiq Noun Dictionary*, for which the Dalai Lama provided a foreword. Myths retold in this novel are from the author's *The Raven and the Totem* and *A Cycle of Myths*.

Contents

EVERY SUMMER, AWAKENED BY some imperceptible signal, a shining multitude of salmon leave the churning depths of the Pacific and return to Alaska to spawn and die. And in their own annual ritual, fishing vessels launch out of safe harbors to meet the migrating schools, which swarm homeward through cold waters, using stars, the moon, and nearly forgotten scents to guide them home, as they have done unerringly since the beginning of time. Just as storms and rough seas imperil the fleets, danger lurks for the salmon at every stage of their journey. All life at sea is precarious. Nothing rests easily. The massive schools must avoid salmon sharks, pods of killer whales, and long, ensnaring nets. And when the dogged salmon reach the mouths of freshwater rivers and streams, waiting impatiently for the incoming tide to boost their one-way race upriver to die, terrible dangers still confront them. Even when the tide has launched them into the familiar flowing waters of their birth, they can only hope to escape the teeth and claws of ever-hungry bears, the talons of vigilant eagles, and the flailing lines of hopeful fishermen. Vigilance, hunger, perseverance—the driving forces in all nature, from salmon to fishermen.

All'inguq

(One)

A long time ago, in a small village nestled along the banks of a river where it emptied into the sea, three brothers hunted and killed squirrels for the fun of it. They hung the tiny furs to dry and collected the bushy tails. They had killed so many squirrels that each day they had to go farther and farther away from the village to find more.

All around the *Erin Elizabeth* the shadow-blackened sea dipped and rose in the cold rain, the canyons between waves narrowing and widening beneath dark clouds swirling on a grey, thundering horizon. Among the great swells the fishing boat looked tiny and lost. On the pitching deck, Seth Evanoff clung to the railing, trying to steady himself and to keep from falling overboard. At sixteen, he had not yet developed his father's sea legs. His feet gave out beneath him when a rogue wave swashed across the deck, dashing a large, plastic tub against the starboard side. He watched in awe as a gust snatched the empty tub and hurled it tumbling into the tumultuous, sloshing sea.

Everywhere, fierce, wind-riven whitecaps were sliding across the bay, which was surrounded by rocky shores and steep, treeless mountains. Many still had snow on their cloud-tangled peaks, despite the warmth of an early Alaskan summer. The slashing wind carried the sound of waves breaking on the nearby shores scudding across the bay. Behind each foam-tumbling crest, endless waves piled up in the distance, mounting and rolling.

A net full of waggling salmon swung wildly above an open hold as the intrepid, forty-two-foot vessel bucked on the jostling waves and lurched sideways from the weight of the laden net. Screeching seagulls hovered above the whitecaps slapping to the port and starboard. At the bow of the blue-and-white boat, a golden retriever, his paws finding little traction on the slippery deck, barked at the noisy birds, sea spray blasting him each time the slicing bow plunged headfirst into the swells and white-tipped waves.

At the stern of the heaving craft, a man was deftly working the control levers to the boom winch, trying to guide the hoisted net into position, while a lean, old man with iron-grey hair hunkered on the deck beside the hold, trying to steady the swaying net by himself. His gnarled fingers clutched the net strings. His feet were planted far apart, his knees bent firmly against the jostling motion.

All three fishermen wore yellow raincoats, the bright rubber made slick by rain and sea. The fronts of the slickers were stained with fish blood.

Uncertain what to do, Seth tried to regain his balance as he stood beside the wiry old man. The teenager was considerably overweight, obese even, and, unlike the old man, unsteady against the boat's roll. It had been a long time since lunch, and Seth was starving. With a free hand, he pulled a candy bar and two packets of slender meat sticks called Slim Jims from a damp raincoat pocket and was deciding which one to open first, when the man working the levers shouted at him.

'Seth!' the man yelled above the din of the torrent, the squawking seagulls, and the cranking winch motor. 'Put that away! You're always eating junk food. You'll ruin your supper! Make yourself useful! Help Lucky with the net!'

'Yes, Dad!' yelled the teenager, quickly stuffing the snacks back into his pocket and pulling down his baseball cap, which was almost blown away by the gales whipping the surface of the sea into a fury, singing through the tight wires, ripping the foam to lace.

The bulging net, still slowly angling above the gaping square mouth of the half-filled hold, swayed with the boat's rocking.

'Grab on, Seth!' his father shouted again. 'Muscle! Use your muscles! Pull!'

When the boy was unable to help the deckhand steady the treacherously swinging net, his frustrated father ran over, took hold of it roughly, and, together with the old man, manhandled it above the hold.

'Can't you do anything right? Hold it like this,' his father snarled before returning to the controls to release the catch.

When the bottom of the net was finally opened, spilling its contents into the hold, some salmon missed the opening and flapped wildly about the deck. It was Seth's job to catch them one at a time and toss them in with the rest of the fish.

Jack Evanoff, Seth's father, had been a commercial fisherman all his life. His own father had been a fisherman. He had worked hard for years to save enough money to buy the boat, and he saw his hold full of fish as a means to pay his bills, including the mortgage and heating oil, the loan for the boat, diesel for the engine, and the salary of his old deckhand who earned a small percentage of the catch. In addition he had to save for the future because winters were long, and some seasons were leaner than others. Not only were salmon returns unpredictable from year to year, but the market price fluctuated from summer to summer, from species to species. King salmon, also called Chinook, always demanded a good price.

Sometimes, so many pink salmon swarmed into the bays that the price would bottom out, glutting the market—nature's perfect example of the law of supply and demand. In those years, beaches near the outlets of rivers and streams were littered for miles in both directions with decaying salmon, the stench insufferable. Even the bears and eagles lost interest after a certain point. Only crabs would eat the dead salmon once high tides had washed the rot-soft corpses back into the sea. At some point during such years of terrible abundance, you couldn't even give the fish away.

While Seth struggled to collect the slimy salmon, Lucky, the old deckhand, worked with the assured skill that comes from a lifetime of doing something until it becomes second nature. The biting wind blew his long, thin hair across his grey-whiskered face. Neither man spoke. Each knew exactly what had to be done and how to do it, putting away the heavy, empty net with the attentiveness of an artist or surgeon, being careful that the net should not tangle, knowing that a tangled net would mean loss of time and money. The old deckhand's fingers were strong and sunburned. One hand was missing part of a finger from an accident long ago, and his broken nose was a constant reminder of another accident.

Life at sea was dangerous.

People had always called the old man Lucky, which wasn't his real name. No one knew the name his parents gave him.

No one had ever asked.

After tossing the last flapping fish into the near-full hold, Seth watched as his father and Lucky struggled to close the hatch.

'The wind is getting too strong!' Jack shouted to Lucky as they leaned face-to-face, bearing down with all their weight to latch the square lid. 'It's getting too dangerous out here!'

Lucky nodded in agreement.

'Let's go home, Jack!' he replied, rain blowing off at an angle from his crooked nose. The howling wind swept his words over the side of the boat, drowning them in the sea.

After everything was secured, the three-man crew met in the pilot house, their yellow slickers dripping puddles on the floor. The fur-soaked dog curled up on the floor beside them, put his head between his paws and sighed heavily.

'The weather is pretty rough,' said Captain Jack, placing his baseball cap on a wall-hook. 'But I'm worried it's going to get worse. We need to make for port now, while we still can. We've got to get these fish to the cannery.'

Leaning so close to the window that his nose almost touched the glass, Lucky squinted, trying to see through the rolling sheets of water that tirelessly pounded against the glass, trying to smash into the dry cabin. He had been on seas like this many times in his life, and he knew how bad it could get if the wind were to grow much stronger.

'You're right, Jack,' he offered, scratching his scraggly beard. 'Let's stay in the lee of the islands. It'll be safer there. The islands will offer some protection.'

They were all aware of the danger of storms on open water.

Alaska is surrounded on three sides by water: the Gulf of Alaska, part of the vast Pacific to the south; the dangerous Bering and Chukchi seas, which separate Alaska from Siberia; and the frigid Arctic Ocean to the north, the frozen home of polar bears and seals. Alaska has more coastline than the rest of America combined. Thousands of islands—some big, some small—line its southern coast. The Aleutian Islands, with their fifty-seven volcanoes, span over twelve hundred miles westward toward Asia. The Inside Passage bordering British Columbia is lined with over a thousand islands. Prince William Sound, over a hundred miles across, is speckled with hundreds of islands. In the summer, deer and bear swim from island to island foraging for food. It was in these pristine waters that the *Exxon Valdez* tanker ran aground on Bligh Reef, spilling almost eleven million gallons of crude oil and killing an estimated quarter million seabirds and some three thousand sea otters and harbor seals—the world's worst environmental disaster at the time.

From years of experience, Jack knew that even the most ferocious winds during the day sometimes die down in the evening. There's some truth to the nautical expression, 'Red sky at night, sailor's delight.' He knew that if they waited awhile, the sea might calm a little. Sometimes a little is enough. Besides, he was hungry. He and his crew had been working hard since lunch, almost nine hours earlier, and he chose to face a drive home through the stormy night on a full stomach.

Jack glanced at his watch and then at his son who was standing beside him, only a couple of inches shorter.

'Looks like it's supper time,' he said. 'What do you say we make for a cove and have something to eat?'

Seth nodded enthusiastically.

Like most teenage boys, he was always hungry.

Before long, the boat had anchored in a small bay, sheltered somewhat from the tempest, though it still rocked a good deal. Generally, boats would anchor in such safe harbors to outlast bad weather. But storms in the Sound can sometimes last for days, putting at risk a catch like the one brimming in the hold of the boat. The fish can spoil if not delivered in time, a total waste of effort and fuel—a risk most captains are not willing to take. Commercial fishermen are gamblers, sometimes betting lives in how they play their stake.

While Jack cooked supper in the galley, Seth and Lucky sat waiting at the rectangular kitchen table, which, like most things on the boat, was bolted down for safety. Everything on board was rigged for rough seas. The cupboards and drawers were latched to keep them from opening and spilling their contents when the boat tossed and heaved on waves and swells. The stove top had special fixtures rigged to hold pots or pans in place. Even the pictures on the bulkhead—which included a map of Prince William Sound drawn by Seth when he was 12 and still interested in such things—were fastened with screws.

A framed photograph of Seth with his mother and father was fixed on the wall above the table. His mother's fairness was highlighted by his father's darker skin and black hair. Everyone in the picture looked happy. His parents had their arms around each other, with Seth standing between them smiling and holding Tucker, who was then a squirming puppy. That was two years ago. His mother had died in a car accident about a year after the picture was taken.

It was winter.

Seth's parents were coming home from a Fisherman's Association banquet in town when two deer leaped onto the road. His father slammed on the brakes and turned sharply to miss them. So sure-footed at sea, his father lost control on the icy land, and the truck spun wildly, jumped a steep bank, and crashed into a tree. His mother was thrown through the windshield and died instantly. His father suffered only a mild concussion, a couple of minor cuts, and a bruised rib.

Seth blamed his father for the accident, which soon became a wedge between them, sharp as a splitting maul.

Truth be told, Jack blamed himself. He thought of his wife all the time, even while working the levers to pull in the long, heavy net full of shiny, waggling salmon.

While the galley filled with the smells of cooking, Lucky played solitaire, flipping over each card and laying it thoughtfully on one of several face-up rows, absently keeping them from sliding off the table with his flannel shirt sleeve. His cup of coffee kept scooting toward the edge of the table, its contents sloshing with the motion of the boat. Tucker lay on the floor on an oval carpet, occasionally raising his head to look around, sniffing, wondering when the food would be ready. He was always given a little something extra in his stainless steel bowl. Seth played with his handheld video game, leaning back in his chair, wearing earphones, listening to music on his iPod, his eyebrows knit tightly as he stared at the small screen, his thumbs moving frantically. Sometimes his tongue stuck out the corner of his mouth. He was still wearing his dark-blue baseball cap with the words 'Erin Elizabeth' embroidered in gold thread across the front. It was his mother's name and the name of his father's boat.

That wasn't the original name.

For a long time the boat had been called the *Natsalané*, the name of the mythic man who created the first killer whale. But Seth's father changed the boat's name after his wife died. He even painted two bright yellow flowers on the stern, one on each side of her name, the long, green, leafy stems framing the two words. She had always loved flowers, happily spending her summer days tending her flower beds.

'Isn't there something else you can do?' his father asked, standing at the sink and draining water from a steaming pot of boiled red potatoes. His sarcastic tone matched his look of disappointment.

Seth understood the look.

In the year since his mother had died, he had withdrawn from the world, spending most of his time at home in his bedroom playing video games, listening to music, surfing the internet, and ignoring his homework. Consequently, his grades at school had slipped dramatically. His mother had always been proud of Seth's good grades. He had also stopped spending time with his friends and going for long walks with Tucker like he used to. As a result, he had gained a lot of weight.

His father called him 'soft' and 'lazy.'

He was right. Nonetheless, it hurt Seth to hear it. His father used to be proud of him. They used to be a happy family.

Seth didn't respond, remaining intent on his game. Besides, his father had complained about his games a thousand times before, saying things like, 'Why don't you play baseball or something? Go ride your skateboard or your bike. You need to get out and exercise. Why don't you hang out with the other boys your age?' And his father's favorite, 'When I was your age, my parents made me play outside all day until it was time for supper.'

Seth had learned to tune out his father's voice, although he wasn't intentionally disrespectful. He had simply learned to act as if he had not heard him, to avoid an argument.

His father placed three blue plastic plates on the table. On each was a thick serving of salmon, which had been fried in a black cast-iron skillet and had honey drizzled over it. Beside the salmon fillet was a pile of small red potatoes and a heaped serving of green beans.

'You know the rules,' his father said, pointing to the top of his son's head. 'Take off your hat when we eat. And turn off that damn music. It's so loud I can hear it from over here. You'll bust your eardrums.'

Begrudgingly, Seth turned off his iPod and stuffed it into a pocket on his slicker.

While Lucky and his father ate, Seth stared at his plate, rolling a potato back and forth with his fork. He didn't like green beans or boiled potatoes, and he was tired of salmon. He only liked hamburgers or hot dogs or pizza. He rarely ate vegetables. After a few minutes, Seth pushed away his plate, walked over to the cupboards and made himself a peanut butter and jelly sandwich on white bread, first cutting away the thin, brown crust with his pocket knife, a sixteenth birthday present from his father a couple months earlier. The single-bladed knife had originally been his grandfather's, who eventually passed it down to his son. Now it had been Seth's father's turn to give it to *his* son.

When he was finished, Seth wiped the flat sides of the blade against his blue jeans before he carefully closed the folding knife and slipped it back into his pocket.

'You never eat anything I make,' his father said sharply, trying not to yell. 'You always ate whatever your mother cooked. Now all you ever want are peanut-butter-and-jelly sandwiches and microwave pizzas. No wonder you don't have any muscles. No wonder you've gained so much weight. You're so finicky. You wouldn't last a day in the wilderness.'

That was another of his father's favorite sayings.

They had had the same argument a hundred times before, and Seth's response was always the same.

'It's the only thing I like,' he mumbled, sitting down to eat his sandwich.

His father and Lucky shared what Seth had left on his plate, giving the salmon skin to Tucker, who gobbled it happily. Dogs love salmon skin.

After supper, Jack made a pot of coffee and filled a tall,

green thermos with a stainless steel cap. He would need the caffeine to keep him awake during the long night's journey home. He was used to the routine, having done it countless times. He was a strong man who believed in the value of hard work, the kind of man who measured his honor by keeping his word, by following through on plans. Besides, there would be plenty of time to rest after the fish were delivered.

After weighing anchor, the captain climbed up to the pilot house and guided the boat out of the sheltering cove, into the blasting headwind, into the deep troughs, the bow busting through waves, the wind hurling itself at the craft, which suddenly seemed smaller, tiny and uncertain on the frenzied sea. Jack's gamble hadn't paid off: the wind hadn't died down. Even with the throttle nearly wide open and assuming no unforeseen problems, it would take all night to reach home.

Once under way, with nothing left to do but wait, Seth and Lucky climbed into their narrow beds. Lucky read while Seth played his video game. Eventually, both fell asleep. Lucky, used to rough seas, slept soundly. With much less experience, Seth slept only fitfully, tossing and turning in his narrow bed like the restless sea, feeling the threat of nausea.

·　·　·　·　·

Seth awoke with a start.

He lay in his upper-bunk bed at first listening to the relentless rain and the intolerable sound of Lucky snoring. It was so loud it could be heard even above the thunderous din of the storm and the wind as it screamed through the wires of the boom. Something kept rolling back and forth across the floor—one of the marbles Seth used to play with, perhaps. But then he began to wonder whether he had brought Tucker into the cabin when he came in for the night. He couldn't remember. He had seen him in the galley during supper, but afterwards Tucker had followed him and Lucky out on deck to make sure everything was secure for the journey home.

Seth hung his head over the edge of the high bunk, looking for Tucker. He called for him softly, so as not to wake Lucky, who was asleep on the narrow bed across from the bunk, one of his skinny legs exposed from under the blanket.

Seth didn't see the dog anywhere on the open floor or beneath him on the empty lower bunk, where his father slept unless pressed by duties on deck, as on this night. He swung his legs over the side and carefully climbed down the sturdy ladder, gripping the rungs tightly as the boat swayed and heaved. When he was safely down, he knelt to look beneath the bottom bunk. That was where the dog sometimes hid during thunder, which always made him tremble and whimper. He didn't like gun shots either.

He wasn't much of a hunting dog.

Tucker wasn't there; only a pair of tennis shoes, two black rubber boots, and a single white sock with a red stripe.

Worried that his dog was on the deck outside, exposed to the storm, soaking wet and shivering and miserable, Seth quickly put on his clothing and boots, as quietly as possible so as not to awaken Lucky, who never stirred.

26

When he was dressed, he grabbed his baseball cap and his yellow slicker from a hook on the wall beside the door.

Seth stepped out of the dry cabin, leaning against the door hard to close it, catching himself as he almost slipped on the deck, made all the more slippery by the salmon that spilled while being loaded into the hold. Their slime never quite washed away no matter how many times the deck was hosed and scrubbed.

Although it never turns truly dark during summer in Alaska, the sky churned like the sea, grey-black and seething. The stinging rain fell so hard that it hurt Seth's eyes when he looked up, squinting and covering his face with one hand. He had trouble telling where the swirling sky ended and the swelling, white-tipped sea began. Lightning flashed. From where he stood, Seth could make out his father's back in the pilot house. He wished he were back inside where it was warm and dry. And safe. When a large wave slapped the side of the boat, Seth grabbed a deck rail to steady himself. A blasting gust blew his cap from his head, sailing it upward and far from the boat on the shifting winds, before it dove like a hungry seagull into the roiling chaos of the sea.

Suddenly, almost imperceptibly above the din of the storm, Seth heard a high-pitched whimper, almost but not quite a bark. He followed the sound across the deck, calling the dog's name.

'Tucker!' he yelled, trying to steady himself as the boat dove into a rising swell and crashed through the other side, sea spray exploding from each side of the bow. The jolt almost bowled him over.

'Here, boy!'

The howling wind swept Seth's words off the boat like his cap, out across the roiling sea, where they floundered in the swallowing waves.

Seth followed the muffled sound of whining. He only heard it intermittently. He had to listen carefully, turning his head toward the direction of the sound. Following a clap of thunder that split the air, he again heard the sorrowful whining. He moved slowly in the direction of the noise, hanging onto whatever steadfast support he could find. At the stern was a stainless steel table bolted to the deck where the crew worked on the nets. Seth bent down and looked beneath it.

There was Tucker, curled up and trembling, his drooping face soaking wet and pitiful.

'Come on, boy,' said Seth, grabbing the dog's collar and tugging. 'Let's go inside where it's warm and dry.'

He dragged Tucker out from beneath the table, but when they had walked only a couple of steps toward the cabin, a large wave suddenly struck the side of the boat, and a wall of seawater swept boy and dog across the deck and over the starboard side. At first Seth was turned helplessly in the dark foam, rigid with panic, unable to determine up or down. He hadn't taken a deep breath before the wave snatched him, and he felt his lungs trying to gasp, to suck in air. He struggled to swim to the surface. When his head finally popped out of the sea, he screamed in reverse, taking in a chest full of water.

Shaking the hair from his eyes, he looked around for Tucker.

'Tucker!' he yelled as whitecaps crashed over his head, making it hard for him to breathe or shout. 'Tucker!'

He couldn't see very far. His body rose and plunged on the crests and valleys of each wave.

The boat was still close enough for Seth to see the two yellow flowers framing the name on the stern, *Erin Elizabeth*. He called out, desperately waving one arm, frantically trying to keep himself afloat with the other.

'Hel . . .! Help!' he tried to scream, but briny water choked his words.

The boat kept going, crashing into the waves, its propeller churning the darkened sea, the distance growing between them, grey and rain-drenched.

Seth turned to look again for his dog, treading the water as he spun about. When lightning flashed, he saw Tucker's head, not too far away, but only for an instant at the peak of a swell before he disappeared. Seth swam for it, struggling against the twisting currents, the pelting torrent, and the surging waves. He could feel his muscles stiffening from the icy water.

Seth knew how dangerous Alaskan waters can be. He had heard stories how even the strongest swimmers can't last long in the frigid northern seas, even during this, the warmest season of the year. When he was close, Seth grabbed the dog's collar, careful not to pull his head below the surface and, at the same time, spoke to him, calming him and encouraging him.

'Are you okay, boy?' he asked, swallowing and coughing up a small portion of the sea, trying to reassure the frantic dog, whose wide eyes sparked with fear.

For a long time they bobbed on the surface, the thrashing sea heaving and scudding around them, tossing them about like lost buoys. At times, the waves seemed to rise up, sharp and angular, like fins or jagged teeth. Seth had to use both arms to tread, trying to stay close to his struggling dog. He had learned long ago to keep his fingers close together, paddle-like. Spread fingers were useless when swimming or treading water.

He could no longer see or hear his father's boat.

It could be miles away by now, he thought, noticing for the first time his bone-deep trembling and that he could no longer feel his toes. His arms were getting tired. He felt dizzy and exhausted.

Seth began to wonder how much longer he could stay afloat.

Atel'ek

(Two)

The brothers, on the edge of becoming young men, had for-
gotten one of the most important values of The People of the
village—the respect of nature, to take only what one needs
and nothing more. One day, the oldest of the brothers was
hunting alone far from home when he saw a squirrel running
along the trunk of a tall tree.

J ust when Seth thought he didn't have enough strength
to stay afloat any longer, he saw a tree, maybe half the
length of his father's boat, tossing on the waves, its leafy
branches rising from the sloshing sea, waving on the wind
like a beckoning hand.

Boat captains in the Sound always have to be on the
lookout for trees, uprooted in storms and cast into the sea,
sometimes floating unseen just below the surface.

Hitting a submerged log at full throttle could sheer the

lower half of an outboard motor or ruin a propeller, not to mention punching a hole through the hull. But in this case, it was a godsend. The wind was urging the tree toward Seth and the dog. With his remaining strength, he grabbed hold of Tucker, and with the other hand paddled as best he could toward the unlikely raft. On reaching the tree, Seth wrapped one arm tightly around the trunk, holding Tucker close to him with the other. The buoyant tree easily supported their weight, and boy and dog momentarily rested their weary limbs.

But the floating tree did nothing to warm them. Seth could no longer feel his fingers or toes, and he was shaking uncontrollably, his teeth chattering. He could feel Tucker trembling as well.

He was scared for both of them.

Having grown up in a fishing town in Alaska, Seth knew that Alaska is fraught with danger. Every mile of it screams out that it can kill you in an instant, from the tallest mountains to the barren Arctic tundra, where even polar bears must struggle over vast distances in their tireless hunt for food. Food means energy to heat the body. Every calorie matters. Stories abound about the hardships of life on the Last Frontier. The waters are so cold and help so remote that kayakers and rafters consider them more dangerous and challenging than similar rivers in the rest of the world.

A crab fisherman who falls overboard in the Bering Sea during the winter crabbing season, where the waters are far more treacherous than in the Sound, has little chance of survival. By law, all vessels must carry a survival suit for each crew member, specially designed to trap body heat and maintain buoyancy, most fitted with strobe lights. But frequently, disaster strikes so suddenly that a man has no time to don the lifesaving gear.

The Bering Sea is callous, unsympathetically taking what lives it can, sparing few.

After a while, Seth caught glimpses of a dark, unmoving shape on the horizon, distant but rising above the height of the frigid waves. He squinted hard each time the log rode to the top of a wave crest. It was a small island. And although it was too tiny to have a name on any map, it could have been called Hope.

From where he was, tossed about helplessly, Seth could see several windswept trees, stunted from trying to grow where they had no business growing. But life is like that, always trying new things, new places, resilient, willing itself to exist by stubborn determination and a bit of sheer luck.

And by good fortune, the log with its desperate, clinging cargo, was carried by wind and current toward the island. The distance closed quickly, and soon boy and dog were able to pull themselves up the rocky shore, where the crashing surf pounded them against the stones, pulling them backwards with each retreating wave, as if trying to drag them back into the sea, frustrated by its failure to swallow them whole.

At last, they clambered away from the beach and crawled beneath a tree, its swaying boughs shielding them from some of the rain. Only some. The boughs did nothing to stop the wind.

Though they were finally out of the water, Seth and Tucker shook from hypothermia. The fact that they still shook was a good thing. It meant their bodies were still fighting to stay warm, a last-ditch effort. Only after the trembling stops does the body begin to give up, surrendering to the elements.

Seth knew that he had to get out of his soaking clothes. Though his fingers barely did what his brain told them, he managed with great difficulty to remove his yellow raincoat and his shirt and pants and shoes and socks. He wrung out as much water as he could and then put them back on. Afterwards, he and the dog leaned against the tree trunk beneath the raincoat, huddling close, shuddering, and moving slightly this way or that to hide from the shifting wind. Occasionally, Seth rubbed his arms and legs vigorously, trying to warm them.

He rubbed Tucker, too.

The dog seemed grateful, licking the boy's face when he was done.

The raging night seemed to last forever, but eventually the rain stopped, the wind ended its flailing tantrum, and the sun began to shine through blue spaces between drifting clouds. By noon, the sky was nearly clear, the sea calm, and the summer sun warming. Seth took off his clothes and hung them over low spruce boughs to dry. He lay sleeping in his underwear on a mossy bed beside a sprawled Tucker, the sun raising their temperatures until, though exhausted, they were no longer cold. Occasionally, Seth would stir at some sound, thinking it to be a boat or an airplane or a helicopter. But each time the rescuers were only a seagull or an eagle or a salmon splashing in the water nearby. After each disappointment, he again slept.

Tucker rolled over on his back with his legs in the air looking ridiculously contented.

By late afternoon Seth was rested but hungry and thirsty. He had swallowed a good deal of saltwater the night before, which caused dehydration, among other less comfortable effects such as relentless and explosive diarrhea. Now he was parched. He imagined that Tucker also needed to drink. But the island was very small, barely a dry spot on the edge of nowhere. He had been too cold and too tired to notice its size before. Seth walked from one side to the other—twenty-three paces at the longest point, only fourteen at the shortest. Because of its size, there were no streams or ponds. No freshwater sources. But it had rained all night. Seth determined that some rainwater had surely collected amid rocks, like tiny cisterns. He found a few such places, occasional cupped formations on the tops of ancient rocks with enough accumulated water for him to sip directly from the rough, gritty surface and for Tucker to lap. They were both able to slake their thirst, at least moderately.

To satisfy his hunger, Seth remembered the candy bar and the Slim Jims in his slicker pocket, the ones his father had told him to put away the day before. They weren't much, and they weren't very nutritious to be sure, but it was all he had.

Seth dug into a pocket and pulled out his iPod.

'Ruined,' he thought as seawater poured out of it.

He shook it until the water stopped dripping; then he

set it on a rock hoping that it would dry in the sun and work again.

He reached into the other pocket and found the Slim Jims, still dry in their wrappers. He opened only one meat stick, using his front teeth to tear open the clear plastic package. Tucker stared, his golden-orange head cocked sideways, looking first at the food and then into the boy's eyes, the way dogs look when they are curious or expectant.

He drooled.

Seth shared the meat stick evenly with his dog but decided not to open the candy bar. He would save it and the other Slim Jim for later. He didn't know when rescue would come. Perhaps it would arrive at any minute, perhaps not until the next day since it was already evening. He thought it best to wait awhile, to save it just in case.

Seth looked out over the water, sparkling like diamonds in the sunlight, and saw numerous other small islands nearby, a larger one about a half mile away. Two sea otters swam close to where he and Tucker sat. The floating creatures watched them curiously until the dog got up and barked, scaring them away.

Seth's grandmother, who was born in the Sound—where her parents and their parents and perhaps a hundred generations of her ancestors had been born—had always tried to teach her grandson the ways of her People, including their stories and the words of their language, now more forgotten than remembered.

They call it *Alutiiq.*

Only a handful of elders in the region still spoke it, mostly the very old. Seth had never really cared to learn.

Most of his generation didn't. Even Seth's father hadn't learned. In all fairness, few people born after the 1950s spoke the native languages of Alaska at all. Everything was in English: television, movies, radio, newspapers and magazines, business . . . even schools were taught in English only. In fact, for a long time the government sent native children, Indians and Eskimos alike, to distant boarding schools, sometimes thousands of miles away, where they were punished if teachers caught them speaking a single word of their native language. They said it was for their own good. They had to stop being Indian. Seth's grandmother had once told him that she had had her mouth washed out with lye soap for accidentally saying a single word.

She couldn't remember which word it was.

It wasn't important.

To the younger generations, no one seemed to care if the language vanished, the way all useless things eventually fade away. Like so many of the old ways themselves, Seth's grandmother had also passed into memory.

But suddenly, sitting as he was against the tree watching the retreating otters, the yellow sun's warmth on his face, Seth recalled the word for sea otter that his grandmother had taught him.

Igam'aq.

He repeated the word several times under his breath, carefully pronouncing each syllable: ee-GUM-uk.

It was strange, he thought, that he should remember this word so clearly.

While he sat, awaiting rescue, swatting mosquitoes, Seth

mused about how much he had in common with the character in his favorite novel, *Robinson Crusoe*. Both he and the protagonist had been marooned on an island. If memory served, Crusoe's island was also in the Pacific, albeit much farther to the south. But instead of Friday, Seth had Tucker. He took the parallel only so far, concerned about the rest of the story—the duration of Crusoe's stranding. Seth didn't want to think about that part. He tried to push the thought from his mind, keep his attention focused on listening for the sound of a boat or an airplane.

And then Seth remembered his father's words.

You wouldn't last a day in the wilderness.

Pinga'an

(Three)

A long time ago, a young couple was married in a small village. They were very happy together. The man was a good hunter who had learned well from his father and uncles. The woman was a good wife who had learned well from her mother and aunts.

The *Erin Elizabeth* made port earlier that morning beneath a clearing sky. And while the bay itself was still choppy, the wind whipping up small whitecaps, the surface in the harbor was nearly flat, protected as it was by the seawall, a long barrier made of giant boulders placed to shelter ships and boats inside.

The journey had taken longer than expected because of the strong headwinds and hampering waves, requiring more diesel than usual for the distance. Jack Evanoff pulled back on the throttle, and the boat drifted up to the cannery dock, gently bumping into the cushioning rubber tires. It idled while Lucky cast the bow and stern lines to a longshoreman, who deftly secured the ropes to the dock moorings.

Lucky had been up for the previous half hour. He always seemed to sense when the boat was nearing harbor, waking up just in time to do his job—uncanny in a way. He was quiet as he dressed, trying not to disturb Seth, who appeared to be in a deep slumber on the upper bunk bed. The way the blankets were pulled over the lumps of two pillows gave that impression.

Almost immediately after Jack killed the engine, the longshoremen began the task of unloading the hold and weighing the salmon. This was the industry of the Sound. The same scene was repeated a thousand times over the summer as fishing boats came into the harbor to sell their catch. Small fishing communities like Jack's lined the Gulf. A check would be ready for the captain in less than an hour, its amount based on the weight of the salmon and the day's market price.

'I can't believe you guys were out there last night,' one of the workers said to Lucky. 'All the other boats came in because of the gale warning.'

The old deckhand grunted gruffly and lit his pipe.

'No one's gonna buy rotten fish.'

While the dock workers did their job, Jack Evanoff poured himself a glass of water and swallowed two aspirins. He had a headache from not sleeping all night and from drinking too much coffee. When he was done, he went down to the sleeping quarters to awaken his son.

Jack opened the door and saw Seth's motionless form under the blankets.

'Rise and shine, sleepy head!' he yelled, loud enough to shake anyone from a dream.

He always said 'rise and shine.' It was something his wife had always said.

When the shape did not rustle, he yelled again.

'Come on, lazy butt. Time to get up!'

When the form failed to move, Jack walked over to the bed to shake his son awake, but his hand felt something other than a body beneath the blankets. It gave too easily, too lightly. He pulled back the blankets, exposing two long pillows; their haphazard arrangement had given the impression of a sleeping body.

Jack walked over to the head and knocked on the door.

'Are you in there, Seth?'

When no reply came, he knocked again, a little louder.

'Seth?' he said, leaning closer, turning an ear to the door.

He opened the door slowly and looked into the empty space, barely big enough for the toilet and a pair of feet. There is no wasted room on a fishing boat.

Jack backtracked to the deck and looked up toward the dock, toward the main shore and town. Frequently, Seth and Tucker got off the boat to stretch their legs while the catch was unloaded. Seth and Tucker had nothing to do aboard ship. Jack and Lucky and the longshoremen did all the work. Besides, for Seth and Tucker, the unmoving earth felt good beneath their feet. Seth never really liked being at sea. He didn't yet truly have his sea legs.

Jack looked for a long time, his head and eyes following

the shoreline. Far off he saw someone with a dog walking along the beach near the water. He squinted, bringing the image into clarity. Even from where he stood he could see that it was a woman and a black lab.

Lucky walked by on the dock below, checking the mooring lines, making sure they were fast.

Jack leaned over the deck rail.

'Have you seen Seth this morning?' he asked.

'He was still sleeping when I got up,'

'He isn't in his bed,' Jack replied in a worried tone.

Lucky, bent over and pulling in the slack, was retying the rope on the giant metal cleat. 'Maybe he got off the boat while I was inside the office,' he said, without looking up.

'Yeah, could be,' Jack said with a hint of disbelief in his voice, his eyes following the curve of the beach. 'All the same, I'm going to walk around town and see if I can find them. You stay with the boat. Move it into its slip when they're done unloading. And don't forget the check.'

'Aye, Captain,' replied Lucky, nodding his head, tapping the bowl of his pipe against the bottom of his boot to empty the ash.

Lucky loved using old sailors' terms like that. He had been at sea all his life, since before Alaska was a state, when it was still a territory. He was what they call a sourdough.

Jack Evanoff walked up the long dock and into town, keeping an eye out for his son and his dog. It wasn't a big town. Its main street was actually called Main Street. Most coastal communities are small, perched at the base of mountains on narrow strips of land bordered by the sea, with a population of a couple thousand people, more or less. Most people are employed in the fishing industry.

This town didn't even have a traffic light, though there was talk of getting one.

All summer long, cruise ships anchored in the harbor almost daily, bringing tourists who disembarked and walked around the quaint streets, taking pictures and buying souvenirs in the various gift shops and stores. Some tourists went on glacier tours and others went out on charter boats to catch salmon or halibut or even salmon sharks, a sport that was growing in popularity. Salmon sharks follow the schools of salmon and often reach up to ten feet in length and weigh as much as five hundred pounds. Unofficial sightings have reported some sharks as long as fifteen feet, weighing upwards of a thousand pounds. They look a lot like a smaller, distant cousin of the ferocious Great White, which live far away on the other side of the world.

Jack walked up Main Street looking into storefront windows, stopping to go inside the places he knew Seth sometimes frequented, like the pizzeria with its old, quarter arcade games, a favorite hangout for the local teens.

'Did Seth come in this morning?' he asked the owner, who was chopping onions.

'Heck, Jack,' replied the nearly bald man who looked to be in his thirties. 'I don't even open for another two hours. I was just cutting up toppings.'

'Can you tell him I'm looking for him if he comes in?'

'Sure thing, Jack,' said the man, raking the pile of cut onions into a plastic bowl with the side of his hand.

Jack ducked into several other stores, asking the same question and always receiving the same answer.

No one had seen Seth or Tucker that morning.

No one had seen them in days.

His concern growing, Jack walked briskly back to the harbor and drove his pickup truck the two miles home, thinking that perhaps Seth had caught a ride home with someone. The thought that his son might be so inconsiderate as to go home without telling him made Jack angry.

He clenched the steering wheel harder than usual.

When he arrived, Jack opened the door and yelled.

'Seth! Seth! Are you home?'

No reply. The house was always quiet in the summer. In winter it could be heard breathing whenever the furnace kicked on, blowing warm air into each room.

After a quick search of the house, Jack scribbled a note on a piece of yellow paper, which he taped to the front door, climbed back into his truck, slammed the door, and drove back to town, his thoughts beginning to fill with worry.

Where is my son?

He remembered the last time he saw him: in the galley after supper the night before when he was making the pot of coffee for the long journey home.

Halfway to town, Jack called his boat using the CB radio mounted under the dashboard. Most people used mobile phones, but Jack still liked some of the old ways.

'*Erin Elizabeth*. Come in. Repeat. *Erin Elizabeth*. Lucky, can you hear me?'

Lucky responded.

'Yeah, Jack. Go ahead.'

'Did Seth come back to the boat?'

'No. I haven't seen him. Copy that?'

Jack's thoughts turned to his wife. She was never far away. He wondered what she would have done in such a situation. She was the glue that held the family together. She would have known what to do.

'I copy,' replied the worried father, letting go of the transmit button.

When he arrived in town, Captain Jack walked straight into the Harbormaster's office and called the Coast Guard.

There was only one other place his son could be.

Staaman

(Four)

The squirrel was all white! The hunter had never seen any-
thing like it before. He raised his bow to shoot, but it was so
pretty he could not kill it. The squirrel ran into a hole in the
trunk of the tree, and then it turned around and motioned
for the young man to follow.

Although the sun never completely sets in Alaska during summer, that night Seth noticed that it was lowest over the mountains to the west. Knowing the sun rises in the east, he was vaguely able to reckon the direction home.

Growing increasingly hungry, Seth thought about a slice of pizza from the pizzeria in town. He imagined it with extra cheese, pepperoni, and black olives—his favorite. He knew that Tucker had to be just as hungry, his belly equally tight.

Tucker tilted his head and stared at the pockets on the front of Seth's yellow slicker. He knew there was food inside. He had seen the boy place it there.

Seth rubbed the dog's head, scratching his throat and behind his ears. When he was done, Tucker licked the boy's hand.

But he still gazed forlornly at the pockets.

'I know, boy. I know,' he said, thinking about the meat stick and the candy bar inside the pocket. 'We'll split one in the morning.'

While schools of salmon all pushed on through the night toward their birth streams, driven by relentless instinct, taking no time to rest, the boy and his dog curled up close together. Seth draped an arm over the dog's chest, feeling it swell with each breath, as the constant waves lapped against the rocky shore. Although this windless night was infinitely more comfortable than the miserable night before, neither of the two slept soundly.

· · · · ·

When he awoke in the morning, the rising sun's meager heat on his face, Seth kept his promise, sharing the other Slim Jim with Tucker. He broke the meat stick in half. Tucker swallowed his in one gulp, barely taking time to chew it. Seth ate his slower, savoring each small bite. Tucker watched and drooled the whole time. He didn't understand why the boy still had something to eat while his was already gone.

Dogs don't do fractions.

After the infinitesimal breakfast, the two drank their

fill of freshwater from the little standing pools about the island. It felt briefly good to be full of anything.

For the rest of the day, Seth kept his eyes on the horizon, hoping to see a boat. He kept his ears attuned to any sound in the distance that might mean rescue. But he neither saw nor heard anything that fanned the embers of his hope. All the while he sat waiting, thinking about food, the tide was going out, temporarily expanding the size of his poor and tiny kingdom.

The only other living things he could notice on the island were the seagulls that came to perch on the few treetops, looking over the water for something to eat.

They were hungry, too.

As he listened to them, Seth thought he remembered the word for seagull.

'Na . . . na-something,' he said, trying to recall the other syllable.

Several seagulls waddled along the beach arguing over food, chasing one another away from some meager morsel, their grey-white wings outstretched in a gesture of anger.

'*Naahqwaq*,' he finally blurted, remembering what his grandmother had told him. He could almost see her mouth move and smell what she was cooking in her kitchen that day. Deer soup with potatoes and onions.

Seth rolled the word around in his mouth, his tongue pressed against the back of his upper front teeth, forming the first sound. He practiced saying the word aloud.

Nok-WOK, he said, placing extra stress on the second syllable.

The day was hot and windless. Seth noticed that the

48

small puddles of rainwater were evaporating, so he shrewdly piled spruce boughs over them to shield them from the direct sunlight. In late afternoon—Seth could only guess by the position of the sun—an airplane flew overhead, far overhead. It was a large passenger jet flying five or six miles above the island, a mere silver speck moving against lazy clouds, its long, white contrail streaming behind it, dissipating after a few minutes.

Seth knew that from such a height, his tiny island was little more than a dot, more sea than land. There was no need to jump up and down and wave.

That night, he thought about eating the candy bar. He imagined the delightful taste of chocolate. But no matter how much his empty stomach begged for a piece, he knew he had to wait until the next morning.

Seth remembered what his father had once told him.

'If you get lost in the woods, don't wander away,' he had said one night while they were sitting around a campfire in their backyard roasting marshmallows. 'That'll only make things worse. Stay put so that rescuers can find you.'

It was good advice, generally.

But Seth began to question it. He had been missing for two days now, and he hadn't heard a single boat or small aircraft searching for him.

What if they never come? he wondered.

The question haunted him all night. He couldn't push it from his thoughts, no matter how hard he tried. Surely his father had noticed that he and his dog were missing. Certainly his father would come looking for him or contact the Coast Guard. Besides, there were other fishermen in the

Sound. And yet, he hadn't seen a single boat in two days.

At last, he fell asleep and dreamed of an all-you-can-eat buffet with a soft ice-cream machine. While he slept, Tucker snored and occasionally whined as if he too were dreaming.

In the twilight, a pod of killer whales swam past the island, their tall, black fins slicing the surface, and Seth's stomach, bare as the cupboards in one of his favorite childhood nursery rhymes, rumbled like an earthquake.

• • • • •

On the morning of the third day, the lone inhabitants of the tiny island awoke stiff and hungry. After standing up and stretching his limbs and yawning loudly, Seth sat down beside his dog and finally opened the wrapper to the candy bar. Tucker's eyes were glued to the object in the boy's hands, his pupils as large as black tea saucers. Even his tail stopped wagging, his whole being focused on the thing the boy was holding. As Seth pulled the chocolate bar out of its wrapper, he could almost swear the dog was smiling.

This time Seth gave Tucker his portion in smaller bites, making the breakfast last, taking equally small bites himself, savoring the flavor of the chocolate melting on his tongue.

It was the best thing he had ever eaten in his life.

When the candy bar was consumed and the empty wrapper was licked clean, boy and dog went from puddle to puddle, sipping and lapping the very last drops of water, which, being the dregs, were a mix of moss, dirt, and lichen.

Not a drop of freshwater remained on the island, and

the sky was deep blue and clear. Only a single, fluffy white cloud flitted on the horizon, all alone on the bend of the world. Seth wondered how long they could last without water, appreciating the irony that he was surrounded by countless billions of gallons of sea water, as undrinkable as motor oil.

With nothing else to pass the time, no television or video games or cell phones, Seth and Tucker lounged all day, sitting first on one side of the island and then on the other, occasionally napping. All the while, Seth kept listening and looking for anything out of the ordinary. And while he waited, he kept studying the larger island across the way, rationalizing that because it was so much larger, it most likely had freshwater and maybe even food. There might even be a cabin.

Besides, it was east of their island, in the direction of home.

Talliman

(Five)

The curious hunter knelt and looked within. He saw that it was a house with a great many empty beds. It was a community house for many people, but there was no one inside. It was entirely empty except for the white squirrel that stood in the middle beckoning him to come inside.

By high noon Seth was unbearably thirsty. His barren stomach felt the way he imagined a spent balloon must feel after all its air is released, withered and collapsed on itself. He kept thinking about the far island.

It seemed too far away.

Then, something in the water caught his eye.

A log was floating slowly past his tiny island. He sat watching it, not particularly interested at first. But within minutes the log was more than a hundred yards away, in the direction of the larger island.

Suddenly, a truth dawned in Seth's brain.

The tidal currents.

Twice a day, influenced by the invisible effects of the tugging moon, the tide comes in and out of the Sound. Among and between the hundreds of islands—more than a thousand in the Inside Passage to the far southeast— the tide actually pours itself like a river. In some places, the changing current is dangerously swift and sudden. In many shallow and narrow bays, like Turnagain Arm, the change in sea level creates bore tides, swift tidal waves miles across that race up into the bays.

Seth watched the log for another few minutes. It was almost out of sight, but still floating toward the larger island.

Although his father had warned him to stay put when lost in the wilderness, he probably hadn't considered lack of food or water. Then, too, his home was in that direction. Besides, maybe no one was looking for him in this area. It made sense to work his way nearer to home, closer to where people might be looking for him.

There was little time. The tide would turn. He decided to swim for the larger island, letting the current do most of the work. What the current was doing for that log it could do for him and Tucker. Although he didn't like the idea of being awash on the sea again, Seth committed himself to his plan.

'Come on, boy!' he shouted to Tucker, as he shoved his iPod into a pocket and started to make his way down the rocks toward the sea.

Tucker looked over the bank at the boy scrambling over the giant stones.

Seth clapped his hands.

'Come on! Heel!' he shouted up to the dog, who had a puzzled expression.

He patted his thighs.

'Heel! Heel!'

Tucker didn't budge.

Frustrated, Seth looked for a stick among the rocks. He found one and held it up, as if to throw it into the water.

'Let's play fetch, boy! Fetch!'

Tucker loved the game. He quickly and nimbly worked his way down to the water's edge. Seth threw the stick in the general direction of the other island, and the dog eagerly splashed into the sea, swimming after it, his powerful tail serving as a rudder. Seth swam after him, satisfied that his plan was working and aware that his iPod was again submerged in the corroding sea.

The water was very cold. But when the dog retrieved the stick, he turned around and swam back to the island. That's the way the game was always played.

The boy threw; he fetched.

Seth trod the water, calling his dog.

'Tucker! Here boy. Come here!' he shouted, waving an arm.

But the dog just dropped the stick and shook himself, water spraying everywhere. Then he looked down at the stick and out at the boy, as if to say, 'There it is. Come get it. What are you waiting for? Throw the stick. Stick, stick, stick.'

When it became apparent that Tucker wasn't going to come after him, Seth swam back to shore and threw the stick again. And again the same game repeated itself.

Seth tried a new strategy.

He pretended to throw the stick, and the gullible dog swam after it, circling where he thought it had landed. Seth swam alongside him, took hold of his collar, and led him out to sea, the current pushing them along toward the other island like flotsam.

Halfway across, Seth looked back, still holding onto the dog. The island they had lived on for three days was little more than a fleck. And although he was already tired from swimming, Seth understood that there was no going back. The strong current that so obligingly carried them this far would be against them all the way if they turned back. It would be like swimming up a waterfall. Better, he thought, just to stay afloat and to let the current carry them.

Seth had no accurate sense of time as they bobbed on the waves. He tried to believe that their progress, a little more than half the distance between the two islands, had been only a few minutes, but he knew it had taken much longer. He wished he had noted more certainly when the tide had begun to flow eastward. If it slowed and stopped, could they still make it under their own power?

After what seemed too long a time, Seth grew certain that the tidal momentum was slowing, but they were, by then, quite close to the larger island. He began to swim vigorously, paddling with one hand and helping Tucker stay afloat with the other. Finally, one foot brushed the pebbly bottom, then the other. Little by little, the pair managed to make it to a beach, a real beach, gently sloping and gravelly, not at all like the steep, boulder-strewn shoreline around their last home.

Boy and dog slogged up out of the sea. They made their way up the beach toward a grassy area above the tide line, the high summer sun warming them.

Thoroughly exhausted, they collapsed into the grass and slept for hours.

A low, humming noise awoke them both. It sounded mechanical, like an engine far away. Seth sat up, rubbed his eyes and scanned the sea trying to find the source of the sound. Far off, almost against the mainland, he saw a fishing boat. It was far away, maybe a mile or further. From where he sat, it looked like an ant crawling along the edge of a table. Even the mast of the boom looked like a tooth-pick. Seth leaped up and ran to the water's edge, jumping up and down.

'Over here!' he shouted as loud as he could, waving his arms.

'Hey! Over here!'

The ant of a boat chugged along without altering its steady course.

'Help! Over here!' Seth shouted until the boat finally disappeared behind an island.

He couldn't hear it any longer.

Seth's heart sank like a slowing flat stone skipped on the water.

As disappointed as he was, his hunger was even more urgent. He and Tucker hadn't eaten anything more than a bite in three days, and junk food at that. The first business on their new home was to find food and water.

They started off down the beach. The tide was going out, exposing more gravely beach every minute. Coming around a bend in the shoreline, Seth saw a streamlet emptying into the sea. He ran toward it. Tucker followed. The shallow stream was barely a foot deep and only a couple of feet across, a little wider in some places. Seth fell to his knees, cupped his hands and scooped up the freshwater. Tucker stood in the stream lapping louder than the sea itself.

After drinking their fill, they walked along the stream, Seth wondering if salmon might be in it. About fifty yards up he saw two salmon, side by side, holding steady against the stream—most likely a male and a hen.

That's what they call female salmon, like a chicken that also lays eggs.

Seth jumped into the water, desperately chasing the salmon, trying to catch one. He splashed about, spinning first this way and then that, the streamlined fish darting around his feet, sometimes brushing against his legs. He almost had one, but it flipped out of his hands, and then both fish turned and raced downriver, back into the depths of the sea.

Both boy and dog walked along the beach, thinking about their hunger.

When they came on a large boulder, which was exposed from the low tide, Seth approached it and saw black mussels growing on the rock below the water line. He remembered how his father once ate raw oysters at a restaurant. The slimy meat looked like snot oozing on a half shell. But his father loved them, dousing them first with lemon juice and a dash of hot sauce. His father hadn't gotten sick on them. They were safe to eat. In fact, Seth remembered that his mother had been particularly fond of sushi, raw fish on an oblong-shaped blob of cold, sticky rice.

Seth used his pocket knife to pry several of the mussels from the rock. Then he used the flat of the blade to wedge open the shells. He scraped out the meat, which was gray and green and slimy.

He wished it was a hot dog instead.

And although his stomach didn't particularly care what went into it as long as it was satisfied, Seth had a difficult time swallowing the first bite. He slid it into his mouth, held it there for a while, his tongue trying to avoid its taste and texture. In spite of his consuming hunger, he couldn't make himself swallow. As hard as he tried, he worked even harder not to spit out the slimy presence in his mouth. It felt like big, chewy snot. Nearly gagging, pounding his fists on his thighs, grimacing, his eyes watering, he managed to swallow, struggling against the retching reflex. Eventually, it went down. He ate three more, each requiring the same stomach-turning efforts.

They stayed down.

Then Seth removed several more from the boulder and fed them to Tucker, who actually seemed to like them, eating them greedily from Seth's palm. They stayed at the rock for a while, eating raw mussels, a pile of empty, black shells growing at their feet.

Several seagulls flew overhead, considering what might be left for them.

Seth remembered the word for mussels that his grandmother had taught him. She called them *umyuk*, pronounced just the way it sounds.

Um-YUK.

When the boy and his dog had consumed over a dozen mussels each, they walked back to the shoreline and sat on a great rocky outcrop, looking out over the sea. Tucker sat beside the boy, who placed an arm around the dog's shaggy neck.

Seth remembered the drenched iPod in his pocket. He shook out the water and sat it in the sun to dry. He didn't really know why he kept thinking he could save the thing. There was no chance it would ever work again. And even if by some miracle it did work, he had no way to charge the battery.

Seth laughed as he looked at the device shining in the sun, realizing the absurdity of his unwillingness to give up something so useless.

While the tide was still out, Seth counted over twenty boulders on the exposed coastline. They looked like giant heads stuck in the mud. Eagles rested on some of them, their keen eyes searching the beach for something to eat. So many boulders, each of them crowded with mussels. Food was everywhere.

The sea would provide for them.

Urwinlen

(Six)

One day, the newlywed husband went whale hunting with many other men from the village. As they paddled out to sea in their longboats, the men waved at their loved ones standing on the shore in front of the painted plank houses and totem poles.

S low down,' said the man on the other end of the phone. 'I know you're worried, but it sounds like your son could still be in town, maybe with some friends or a girlfriend. I think it's too soon to call a search.'

'I told you, I already looked for him in town. He's not here.'

'Did you call his friends?' the man asked.

'Well, no.'

'Then I recommend you first check with them, look around town some more and go back to your house. He might be there by now. Maybe he left a message.'

'I guess I could check around some more,' replied the anxious father.

'Good,' said the man on the phone. 'In the meantime, I'll call the Coast Guard and let them know what's going on. They may need to be in on this.'

'All right,' replied Jack Evanoff, promising to call back if he found his son.

For the rest of the day he stopped at the homes of some of Seth's old friends, the ones he used to hang around with before his mother died, before he withdrew into the lonely world of himself. No one had seen Seth or Tucker. Jack drove back to town and stopped to inquire in every single store. Same news. He went home twice, each time greeted by the yellow note he had taped to the door.

By the time someone called from the State Trooper's office, it was already evening. Jack told the officer how no one had seen his son since the day before they left to go fishing. The officer agreed that it was time to begin a search. Because their airplane was down, awaiting a new alternator, which would arrive in the morning, he promised to start as soon as the part was installed.

That night was the second longest night of Jack's life— the other being the night his wife died. He couldn't sleep. Instead, he sat at the dining table looking through photo albums, listening for the telephone or the sound of the front door opening.

Some nights seem to last forever.

· · · · ·

Bright and early the next morning, a small white and

blue-pinstriped Citabria lifted from the runway, banking almost immediately, making the turn westward to follow the coast. Turbulence rattled the aircraft.

'You have any idea where he might have fallen overboard, Jack?' asked the pilot, Leo Walsh, speaking through the microphone on his green headset, which sounded tinny. It was too loud inside the small prop plane to hear without headphones. Like Jack, Leo had grown up in the town. His friends called him Lee. His father had also been a fisherman and a pilot. Lee and Jack had gone to school together, though Jack was a year older. They had even gone bear hunting together. Lee was a big man, six foot one or two, almost too large for the tight cockpit.

'No. I was up in the pilot house driving all night,' replied the anxious father. 'Could be anywhere.'

The plane flew low between the mainland and the islands, pilot and passenger looking out the side windows for anything that might catch their attention. Several times the pilot veered toward something on a beach or floating in the water, but it always proved to be a log or a rusting fuel drum or a rock. When Jack saw something moving along the edge of an island's woods, it turned out to be a black bear scouring the beach.

One of Jack's friends—Bard Young, who had sometimes fished with Jack's father when he was younger—was also aloft in his own plane, a small Cessna, flying about a mile or two ahead of them, close to the mainland. A report had gone out over the air to all boat captains in Prince William Sound to be on the lookout for the sixteen-year-old boy and his dog. Dozens of boat captains responded to say they would help. That kind of response is not unusual in Alaska, a place where nearly all emergencies are matters of life and death, where time is always in control of survival, and where, someday, it may be you that needs help.

What goes around comes around.

Jack Evanoff had paid his dues. Three years earlier he had helped to rescue a deer hunter who had been mauled by a bear. And only the previous fall he had rescued the crew of a sinking boat that had struck a submerged rock, another hazard in the Sound.

He knew the score.

'Over there,' said Jack excitedly, pointing to something on a beach.

Lee steered toward the beach, pushed in gently on the steering yolk, bringing the plane down closer for a better look.

'It's just a beached whale,' he said, when they were close enough to see.

Jack looked out the window. He knew that whales washed ashore are a common sight in the Sound and a giant meal for the world above the waves. Sometimes pods of beluga whales, uniformly white and up to fifteen feet long, swim into shallow bays following schools of herring or salmon. Occasionally, they don't leave before low tide and become stranded on the mud flats, gasping until the incoming tide frees them. In his life, Jack had seen many whales lying helplessly on the tidal flats, their whiteness a stark contrast against the muck. Beluga populations are down in the Sound. No one knows why for certain. But over-fishing may be responsible, at least in part.

John Smelcer

Sometimes Jack felt a little guilty about that.

'Does Seth know how to swim?' asked Lee.

'Yeah, you bet. He's been able to swim since he was five or six.'

Lee looked at Jack and smiled.

'Well, maybe he made it to one of these islands.'

But Jack remembered the sea that night, the storm, the driving rain, the slapping waves, the deep, rolling swells. Knowing that his son could swim across a languid pond didn't comfort him.

'Yeah,' he said weakly, 'maybe so.'

Neither spoke after that for almost an hour. The small plane buzzed over several fishing boats, tilting its wings from side to side as it passed overhead, a familiar gesture like waving a hand.

Boats up and down the Sound radioed in that they hadn't seen anything, giving their locations to aid in the search.

Eventually, the aircraft had to turn back. Wing tanks hold only so much fuel. Lee had to turn around when the fuel gauge reached the halfway mark.

'Sorry, Jack. We gotta head back to town,' he said, knowing the news would be hard for the father. It would be hard for any father.

Jack Evanoff leaned over, looked at the gauge himself, saw the position of the needle. He understood. If they flew any further, they risked adding themselves to the search.

Lee tried to raise his spirits.

'I'll fly on the outside of the islands on the way back, on the seaward side. Maybe we'll see something. What do ya' think?'

Jack nodded and then turned and looked out the window, his eyes following the bends of the shoreline. He didn't think Seth would be on the seaward side of the islands since their course toward home that night had not taken them that way. He was sure his son would be on the inside, but it was worth a look, especially since they hadn't seen him on the way out.

They didn't find him.

A little later, the plane flew its approach into town, dropped flaps and reduced speed almost to a stall, and after a moment the oversized tires touched down on the runway, the craft bouncing once. Lee used the foot pedals to steer the aircraft over to the runway apron and shut down the engine.

'We'll find him tomorrow,' he said, forcing a comfortless smile as he opened his door.

As the two stepped out from the cramped plane, Jack noticed a man standing in the open doorway of a blue metal building. It was Rod Clark, the manager of the town's airport, more airstrip than airport. He seemed to be waving to catch Jack's attention. The man motioned again and began walking toward them.

'Jack!'

'Go ahead,' said Lee, staying behind to tie down the struts in the event of strong winds. The anchors were made from bald tires with cement poured in the middle, heavy enough to keep the craft secure.

Jack walked quickly to the man who had called him.

'Yeah, Rod.'

The man had a stern look on his face.

'I'm afraid I have some bad news.'

Jack's stomach swooped like a seagull about to land on the sea in a hard wind. His heart and lungs felt as though they were being squeezed in an invisible hand. He could barely breathe.

'A boat found Seth's hat.'

'What do you mean?' asked Jack. 'How do you know it's his?'

The man averted his gaze, unable to look the distraught father in the eyes, unable to deal with the furrowed expression on his face. Instead, he looked at his hands while he spoke.

'One of the boats found a blue baseball cap with your boat's name on it, the *Erin Elizabeth*. That was your wife's name, wasn't it?'

The man said nothing after that, letting the words drown in the father's memory of his son.

Jack's eyes welled up, his jaw quivered, an eye twitched. He had to look away—the way all men look away—to keep from collapsing to his knees, his heart unable to take the loss of his wife and his son in such a short time.

Maquungwin

(Seven)

'I cannot come in,' said the young man. 'I am much too big.'
To his amazement, the white squirrel spoke to him. 'Lean
your bow against the Great House and you will be able to
come inside.' The hunter did as he was instructed and to his
surprise he became small enough to walk into the empty hall.
He saw that the white squirrel was actually a beautiful girl
who was wearing a white fur coat. She said to follow her up
to the top of the Great Tree.

After their slippery meal of mussels, Seth decided
to explore the island, which was considerably larger than the last. There was even a small mountain in the
middle, not nearly as tall as the ones across the water on
the mainland, but a mountain nonetheless. As boy and dog
pushed their way through dense brush, Tucker flushed a
covey of grouse, as well as a deer from its resting place.

Seth knew that deer often swim from island to island in search of food.

As the two castaways walked along the shoreline, they came across berry plants—rosehips, low-bush and high-bush blueberries, raspberries and salmon berries—which were still in flower, too early for berries but a forecast of abundance later in the summer and early fall. They even saw bear tracks in the soft soil.

Seth hadn't worried about bears back on the tiny speck of an island, which was too small and barren to conceal a surprise, but here he would have to be wary. Bears roam throughout the islands of the Sound, mostly black bears on those larger islands with salmon spawning streams. In many ways, he knew a black bear is more dangerous than its larger cousin, the brown bear, which can weigh well over a thousand pounds and stand over ten feet tall, with claws as long as kitchen knives. Black bears are smaller but dangerously unpredictable.

Seth picked up a piece of grey driftwood, about five feet long and nearly as thick as his wrist. A feeble defense, to be sure, he thought, but somehow carrying the staff gave him a little more confidence.

When it was late, Seth and Tucker returned to the shallow stream to make camp. He decided it was the best location. The beach was wide and clear of brush and trees, and it would be easier for a boat or an airplane to see them. Besides, he already knew there was food during low tide, and the stream would provide drinking water, maybe even salmon.

And something else occurred to him. This was the inward side of the island, facing the mainland. He recalled that his father's course toward home that night took the inside passage, not the seaward side. Seth considered that his father would most likely concentrate his search there.

Seth rummaged along the shoreline, collecting driftwood to build the frame of a lean-to. He would build it on the grassy area far above the high-tide line, which was clearly marked by a swath of jumbled debris washed ashore during high tide by wind-driven waves. He even found bits of rope, lost, most likely, from fishing boats. He used the various lengths to lash the driftwood poles together. The rickety structure fell over several times, frustrating Seth, until he figured out the basic engineering, how to brace one side against the other, making it sturdy.

When he was satisfied that the structure was strong enough, grabbing both uprights and rattling the framework, Seth broke low-lying limbs from evergreen trees and piled them atop the lean-to—a spruce-scented barrier to keep out whatever weather it could: rain, wind, or sun. He gathered extra boughs to make a comfortable bed for himself and Tucker.

That night, Seth and Tucker awoke to a commotion. They could hear splashing in the nearby stream.

Bears.

Peering out from the lean-to, Seth saw a black bear and her two cubs wading in the water trying to catch salmon, which were racing upstream on the incoming tide.

Tucker growled and whined, while Seth held him back by his collar and covered his muzzle to quiet him.

'Easy, boy,' he whispered, hoping the bears wouldn't notice them in their little defenseless shelter.

Seth knew that a mother bear can be very dangerous, protective of her offspring. Many maulings in Alaska are caused from sudden encounters when a hiker or fisherman inadvertently comes between a sow and her cubs. Her motherly nature to protect her cubs is as strong as her instinct to sleep away the long, dark winters.

While the bears were busy trying to catch fish, the boy and his dog quietly slipped from the lean-to and stole away into the nearby woods, spending the rest of the night wide awake, nervously watching the bears from a safe distance.

Downwind.

· · · · ·

The next morning, after the bears had gone off to sleep away the warm day, Seth dismantled his shelter and moved it further away from the creek. He had relearned an important lesson: It's never a good idea to pitch camp along a spawning stream in Alaska in the summer. It's like pouring kerosene on a fire to put it out. Seth remembered something his father once told him when they were deer hunting.

'Everyone makes mistakes, but some mistakes don't come with a second chance.'

After reassembling the makeshift home, Seth was hungry. He walked over to the creek, which had a good many salmon in it. At first he tried to catch them like the bears, chasing them vainly. That approach didn't work. He stood studying the water, noting the shallow sand and gravel bottom and how the banks narrowed in places.

An idea lodged in his brain.

Seth used stones to build a dam across the creek, upstream, not to hold back water from pouring to the sea, but to block the progress of salmon swimming upstream. Then he built another one a little further downstream, leaving an opening just wide enough for the salmon to swim through, a sort of corral for fish. He placed a few extra stones on the bank near the opening. Then he walked along the shore to the mouth, careful not to startle the fish He stepped into the creek and began walking upstream, splashing loudly as he waded along, scaring the salmon upriver. Some fish turned and darted past him back into the sea, but most escaped ahead of the boy, swimming through the stone gate. All Seth had to do was set the final stones in place, effectively trapping them in the weir.

With no place to go, they could more easily be caught, though as slimy as they are, they were still difficult to grab.

Tucker tried to catch his own.

One fish, caught in some ripples, slapped the dog in the face with its tail.

Tucker got a shocked surprise, and Seth got a laugh, his first since their ordeal began. Eventually Seth caught a salmon, scooping it up in his arms, holding the fish against his chest while it wiggled and flapped. He quickly tossed it far up onto the bank and then clubbed it dead with his walking staff.

Tucker licked the still fish.

'Hold on, boy,' said Seth, kneeling, gently pushing away the dog, and pulling his pocketknife from his pocket.

'Let me cut it up first.'

Like any fisherman, Seth knew how to fillet a salmon.

He had helped his father do this many times. He carefully made a slit just behind the gills and then worked the thin blade along the back, slowly peeling the deep red meat from the spine bones. He did this to both sides. When he was done, he rinsed the two halves in the creek, washing sand and slime from them. Tucker chewed on the carcass, eating much of it, while Seth gathered wood to make a fire. When he had a pile of dry wood and tinder, Seth vigorously rubbed two sticks together, trying to create a spark, the way he had seen in movies. He knew that a fire could also be used to make a smoke signal to attract the attention of rescuers. After a long time, without even the faint hint of wood smoke, Seth tried another method. He collected various rocks from the beach and struck them against each other. He had seen that in the movies as well.

That didn't work either.

The unimpressed tinder lay in a small heap, no warmer than the sun's rays falling on it. Tired and hungry, Seth decided to eat the salmon raw. If his mother could eat sushi made with raw tuna and salmon and octopus and other fish, then he could eat his hard-won catch uncooked. It wasn't as bad as he thought, though it was mushy, not at all firm and flaky the way it was when his father grilled it, drizzling honey or barbecue sauce over the fillets. He took small bites, cautiously waiting between bites for a verdict from his stomach—in or out. It seemed the judgment was favorable.

The fish stayed down.

As always, Seth shared his food with Tucker.

While they ate, the several uncaught salmon splashed in their pen, searching for a way out.

When they had finished eating their lunch, Seth noticed that the tide was going out, exposing the dark sea bottom. He had seen movies in which people spelled out S. O. S. in large letters with whatever was at hand. He hastily gathered light colored rocks and spelled out the universal signal, thinking a plane flying overhead would be able to see it. He waited nearby on the beach for the rest of the day, hoping that they would soon be rescued. While waiting, he and Tucker took a nap, tired as they were from staying awake all night watching the bears. Little by little, hour by hour, the tide turned, poured inland, and drowned the stone-spelled letters.

Only the fish and scuttling crabs would read it.

Eventually, the sun slid down its dipping angle, and dusk arrived. The sow and her cubs came out from the forest and found the rest of the trapped salmon—an all too easy meal.

Seth watched from a distance as they ransacked his little fishery, wondering if they would eat all the fish. He hadn't considered the bears returning. He should have opened the weir, not because he could have saved the salmon, like canned goods in a pantry, but because now the bear would return to this spot along the stream as if it were her own.

No matter, he thought, *more salmon arrived on every tide, and the stream is long enough for me and the bears.*

For the rest of the night, he lay beside his dog inside the shelter, sleeping fitfully, listening to the sound of the earth and the sea and the sky, clutching his iPod as if his life depended on it. For the first time, Seth realized that he didn't miss his loud music or his noisy video games. He hadn't even thought about television.

The sound of nature was all around him, tranquil and beautiful and alive. It spoke to him—a voice he'd never before heard.

Sometimes the most important things find us when we're not even looking.

Inglulen

(Eight)

When they arrived in a room at the top of the Great Tree, an old man dressed like a chief spoke to him.

'I have been waiting for you to come. Why have you killed all of my people?' he asked, his voice filled with a great and heavy sadness. 'All of my children and grandchildren are gone except for my favorite granddaughter who led you to the Great House. Why have you done this?'

Seth awoke alone in the morning. Tucker was gone from his side. The boy crawled out from his shelter and whistled, turning each time so the shrill sound would carry in all directions.

'Tucker!' he yelled. 'T-u-c-k-e-r!'

At first Seth thought the dog might have gone to do his business in the bushes. But after calling for him for several minutes, he began to worry. There was no telling how long his companion had been gone, perhaps many hours. He couldn't remember the last time he felt him by his side. He walked along the water's edge, looking far up and down the beach, stopping occasionally to shout the dog's name.

After walking a long distance, Seth began to wonder if the mother bear had got his dog. Perhaps the sow had attacked him for coming too close to her cubs. Perhaps they were eating him even now, hidden in thick alders, the sound concealed by the din of the burbling creek. The image made the hair on the back of Seth's neck bristle. Goose pimples formed on his arms. And although he was only sixteen, Seth understood that life is that which dies; life is only the exclusion of death.

But then he thought that he surely would have heard some ruckus, the barks and growls and yelps of a deadly struggle. The realization that nothing of the sort had startled him awake was heartening, giving him some measure of hope, albeit small.

As Seth walked along the beach, fearing that he might be alone, he suddenly thought about his mother. He missed her terribly. They had been a close family, more so than most. He remembered how when he was a little boy his parents used to sit in bed with him, one on each side, reading to him before bedtime. When they were finished, they would tickle him, pull the sheets up to his chin, pat him gently on the chest, kiss him on the head saying how much they loved him, before turning out the light. In the dim-lit hallway, he would watch his father embrace his mother, kiss her on the cheek. He always fell asleep wrapped in their love, even on snowy winter nights when the wind blasted against the rattling windowpane.

Seth stopped walking to wipe his eyes and cheeks with a shirt sleeve.

By mid afternoon he was hot from walking all over the island, searching for his lost dog. Seth smiled as he thought how people *outside* mistakenly imagine Alaska as a frozen wasteland whose inhabitants dwell in igloos surrounded by penguins. For one thing, penguins lived on the other side of the planet. Truth is the highest temperature on record in Alaska is 99 degrees! Many summer days, especially in the interior, approach 90. It is so warm that even pestering mosquitoes take refuge from the sun.

Seth decided to take a swim in a cove, where a little piece of the sea was briefly captured by the land. He stripped off his clothes and stepped into the cold water. It felt good to be cold. But he couldn't help remembering how his feet and arms had grown numb in the cold sea when he and Tucker had struggled to stay afloat during the storm.

He swam out a couple of hundred feet from shore, turned over on his back, and floated lazily, looking up at the sky, as blue and deep as the sky in a child's crayon drawing.

A strange noise disturbed the peacefulness around him. It sounded like air suddenly released under pressure, the way a bus sounds when the doors open. Then he heard it again and again. Seth rolled over, treading water, turning to look for the source of the noise. Several killer whales were behind him, closing in. He could see the tall, black fins slicing the taut surface.

One fin looked to be four feet high, maybe more.

Seth panicked.

He spun around and tried to out-swim them to shore, an impossible feat. Almost nothing in the sea swims faster than a killer whale. He was so terrified that his form was sloppy and he slashed wildly more than swam. In a moment, the whales were upon him, coming so close he could have touched one. Seth stopped flailing as the four whales encircled him. He could see their black and white patterns, their black eyes sizing him up, their sharp ivory teeth.

Seth knew that killer whales hunt in packs like wolves. In fact, they are called sea wolves. Marine biologists have seen them hunt giant whales, taking vicious bites, trying to kill the larger whales by riding on their backs, using their weight to drown them. Whales have sometimes been found washed ashore, whole portions of them missing, seagulls pecking at the wounds.

As Seth waited for the inevitable, he suddenly recalled a story his grandmother had told him. It was the story of the first killer whale. In the story, a man named Natsalane' carved a whale from a red cedar log. His grandmother had pronounced the man's name: Not-SAY-law-nay. He pushed the carved shape into the sea, where it transformed into a killer whale with its mouth of sharp, white teeth. The man told his creation to kill his enemies in their distant canoe, who had tried to kill him. He watched from shore as the killer whale raced toward their canoe, capsized it, and killed the men aboard, ripping them to pieces, turning the sea red. He could hear their screams. When it had finished its task, the whale returned to its master, awaiting further commands. Terrified of the awesome ferocity of his creation, the man told it to never again kill people. And, so the story goes, killer whales have never attacked people since.

Seth didn't know if it was true.

It was just a story.

Nonetheless, he spoke to the whales, his voice breaking from fear.

'You won't eat me, will you?' he said. 'Please don't eat me.'

He kept pleading with them, hoping they would realize he wasn't a seal or sea lion.

This time, when they came close, he reached out and let his hand pass along the length of their lithe bodies, feeling the smoothness of their skin. He could feel their sleek forms, their sheer power. They were beautiful, a force of nature.

They were nature.

After a while, the whales turned and swam back out to sea. Seth paddled to shore, sat naked on the gravel beach, warming under the sun, drinking the wild air, and watching until their fins were too far away to see. He held his arms across his chest, afraid he was going to cry with relief. Instead, he heard himself laughing, at first quietly, to himself, then louder and louder until his joyful voice thundered across the bay.

No one will believe me, he thought.

And he was probably right.

• • • • •

That evening Seth caught another salmon and tried to

make a fire. Once again he used various sticks and stones, varying his technique. No matter his persistence, not even the ghost of a wisp arose from his labor, and once again he ate his fish raw.

That night a stiff wind arose, and Seth slept alone curled up in his shelter with his yellow slicker draped over him. He worried about Tucker all night, sitting up a dozen times, thinking he had heard a bark from far away, fluttering along the beach like a leaf on the wind.

The next day was calm and sunny. Seth walked around the island in the other direction, forcing his way through almost impenetrable brush where the beach ended, calling for his dog, and worrying about bears. While ensnared in the woods' dense alders more than a hundred yards from the shore, Seth heard an airplane. He stopped to listen, trying to determine its direction. He forced his way through the brush, stumbling, branches slapping him in the face. By the time he emerged on the beach, the plane had already passed. The boy stood and watched until it became as small as a mosquito buzzing on the horizon, hoping it would turn around.

But it never did.

After an exhausting day, Seth finally returned to his camp near the salmon stream, the only freshwater creek he had encountered on the island. And there, sleeping on the yellow raincoat spread over his mattress of spruce boughs, was Tucker. When the dog heard the boy's footsteps on the gravel, he raised his head and pricked his ears. When he saw who it was, Tucker bolted down the beach, kicking up small rocks, his ears flopping as he ran. Seth dropped to a knee, and with the biggest smile he ever made, held his dog to him, kissing his hairy face, rubbing him everywhere.

Qulnguan

(Nine)

The Indian looked around and saw that this room was also empty, and then he answered the old, sad chief. 'I have not killed your people. I have never killed a person in my life. I do not know what you are saying, old father.'

'Look around you,' said the chief. 'See how we are alone here now where once these halls were full of my people.'

The young man looked again and replied, 'But I did not kill anyone.'

A week had passed since the night of the storm. Seven days without television or video games. Seven days without music, cell phones, or pizza. Seven days away from his comfortable home and his father.

Seth began to worry. Until this point, he had been certain that he was simply biding time, awaiting rescue, which would arrive at any moment—another boat, this time closer, motoring around a bend; a plane flying overhead, lower, looking for him on a beach. All he had to do was stay alive during the tedious hours between *lost* and *found*. Now a notion began to creep into his mind, slyly, the way a lynx stalks a rabbit—the troublesome thought that after a week any ongoing search for him might be called off. To the once-searching world of home, he might be dead.

Seth tried to shake away the worrisome consideration from his mind and went out at low tide to scrape mussels from the giant, exposed boulders. While he worked, low gray clouds rolled in across the sea, from the south, and tangled in the green mountains on the mainland, barely visible through the increasingly heavy air. A soft, misty drizzle fell from the gloomy sky, light as a cool breath, a whisper of the rain shortly to come.

When Seth and Tucker returned to camp, retreating from the incoming tide, the lean-to was destroyed, its driftwood supports and crossbeams strewn up and down the beach, spruce boughs everywhere. Tracks in the sand told the story. The mother bear had followed the scent of the boy and the dog, perhaps worried that the strange smell might represent some peril to her cubs or competition for the fish.

Perhaps she was just curious.

Either way, she and her cubs had wrecked the shelter.

Just then, as Seth stood looking about him, wondering how to put it all back together again and if he should move it to a safer distance, it began to rain—a heavy, thunder-ous downpour that fell with such intensity that Seth could barely see ahead—a deluge so torrential it reminded him of the story of Noah and the Flood. The sea seemed to be filling up with rain. Much of the southern coast of Alaska, especially the southeast, as it pours down the edge of northwest Canada, forms Alaska's Tongass National Forest, the wettest place on the continent.

Seth ran into the woods, looking for shelter. He chose a large spruce tree, its wide green limbs blocking a fraction of the downpour. For the rest of the day and into the night, he sat against the trunk of the tree, Tucker curled up beside him, the incessant rain loud on the hood of his slicker. They were miserable, sitting hunched in the teeth of the world, their hardship keen as an axe, heavy and biting.

Seth's spirit wilted.

Tucker's face drooped.

'I'm sorry, boy,' said Seth, looking at his unhappy companion squinting up at him. 'There's nothing I can do.'

To add to his misery, Seth had to go really bad. Peeing wasn't a problem, but he hated the other business, especially in a downpour. Usually, when he went camping with his family, they brought rolls of toilet paper, kept dry in plastic bags. But here, stranded in the wilderness without any conveniences, Seth had to use whatever was at hand: leaves, dry grass, seaweed, pine cones.

Pine cones were the worst.

Seth began to think of home, shuffling through his memories—the way Lucky shuffled his worn-out playing cards—flipping them over and laying them out one after the other on the table of his mind until he came upon a particular memory, brought on most likely by the rain.

It was a recollection from when he was ten or eleven. One cloudy summer afternoon, just before the fishing season, his father had taken the family on a boat ride to an island. He moored the boat in a small cove, and the family hiked along a path up a steep hill, his father carrying a wicker picnic basket. Sometimes he let his son carry it. It was so heavy and unwieldy that Seth had to use both hands, holding it against his waist as he wobbled along. At the top of the hill his mother spread out a green-and-white checkered blanket, a classic picnic accessory, like the wicker basket.

The three enjoyed their happy lunch of cold fried chicken, potato salad, apples, and grapes—talking, telling jokes, and laughing. When they had finished eating, his mother stood at the hill's edge, looking out over the sea, their blue-and-white fishing boat floating patiently far below. Seth's father crept up behind her, wrapped his arms around her waist, and kissed her on the neck. They stood that way for a long time—a mother and father, husband and wife—holding onto each other and the memory of that moment while their son sat on the blanket watching them, trying to understand that kind of love, feeling its warmth as from a campfire.

Just then it began to rain.

The small family hastily packed their belongings and dashed down the trail to the boat, sliding in the mud, laughing as they occasionally slipped to the seat of their pants. When they finally made it to the boat, all three were soaked and muddy. His father insisted on taking a photograph of Seth and his mother.

In it they were both smiling.

Seth could still remember the laughter.

The rain hadn't ruined their day, couldn't ruin it. Some things are indestructible, the way memories never change. Only we change. The world changes.

Everything changes.

Sometimes Seth locked himself in his bedroom and sat for hours holding the photograph, listening to music, touching her face through the smudged glass.

The bone-deep memory only increased Seth's misery. He was all alone, save for the drenched and droop-faced dog beside him. He was cold and empty. For the first time during his ordeal, Seth was really frightened, not a fear like being left alone in the dark or of an unnamed thing hiding beneath the bed or waiting in the wardrobe, but a dread of being alone, perhaps of dying alone. For the first time, hope slipped from him, made slippery by the rain. The loneliness beat down upon him like the never-ending rain, cold and eroding.

Seth began to cry.

He rested a wet hand on his wet dog and wept for a long time. It is a deeply personal place, the desolate country of tears. He wanted to cry out for his mother, the way grown men sometimes want to cry out for their mothers, especially in times of despair—the way some religious men, near the hour of their demise, call out to the beloved mother of another man who was once lost in a wilderness and who died a long time ago.

Home seemed far away, separated by more than distance and sea. All through the insufferable twilight he tried to sleep, but sleep was impossible. Exhaustion aggravated his fear, compounded it, and gave it even more edge.

Seth suddenly looked up and saw a raven hunkered before him on an old, broken tree limb. His black head was cocked sideways, his black eyes blinking against the rain, staring at the boy, as if pleading to share his yellow slicker. To Seth, the raven looked every bit as miserable as he and his dog. When it became apparent that he was not to be invited, the raven shook his black feathers and flew away, cawing his discontent, cursing the bursting clouds.

Caw! Caw! Ga-gok!

As he watched the black bird evaporate into the sodden greyness, Seth recalled stories his grandmother had told him about Raven, a god-figure in their culture, more cruel than kind, more Destroyer than Creator, though he is always both. An enigma. A Trickster. Stories of Raven appear in every culture in Alaska, as common as the ubiquitous birds themselves. They are true survivors, perfectly adapted for the hardships of life in the Far North. One of the stories Seth remembered from his grandmother was about Raven and the first salmon. Because salmon are such an important resource to the People, there are many stories about them, mostly about their creation and about respecting them. She told it to him one day while they were cutting salmon to smoke and can. In the story, salmon could only float on the surface of water when Raven first made them—easy meals for bears and eagles. So, Chief of the Salmon People pleaded with Great Raven.

'Please help us,' he implored, after telling Raven of their plight.

Raven thought and thought, and then he cut a slit in the Salmon Chief's head and placed two small stones inside.

From then on, all salmon could swim deep, escaping teeth and talons.

As proof of the myth's truth, Seth's grandmother cut a salmon head in half, laterally, between the nostrils and the eyes. Smiling broadly, she showed her grandson the two small, gray stones, exactly where Raven had put them. Seth understood that it was really the brain, but he could understand the association.

Seth remembered the word for raven. He had heard it many times, perhaps more often than any other word his grandmother had taught him.

Abalanaq.

He voiced the word several times, trying to get the pronunciation just right.

Ah-BOLL-in-nok.

· · · · ·

Sometime after dawn the rain ceased, the fog dissolved, and the low sun glared through disentangling clouds, shining on a patch of yellow flowers, the world smiling. Morning was still yawning when Seth picked himself up and stretched his limbs, beads of water sliding down his yellow slicker, the tiny rivulets soaking into the already rain-drenched ground. The constant patter of rain on leaves and on the hood of his slicker was followed by a silence as crisp as the newly burst sunshine piercing into the empty spaces between clouds. Just then a small, black-capped chickadee alit on a trembling branch and began to sing the welcoming song of morning.

Seth listened for a while. For the first time he understood

that given the right moment, everything is extraordinary, even in despair. Then he walked down to the beach near the lapping water's edge, followed closely by Tucker, who stopped several times to shake himself dry. Mist arose from the warming beach stones, made black from the rain. Salmon rolled and splashed in the languid sea. Seth faced the eastward rising sun, the direction of home, running a hand over his face and chin, feeling the course stubble of a new beard. He realized he hadn't shaved since the morning the boat had left the harbor. That had been ten days earlier.

Suddenly, Seth understood what he had to do. No one was coming for him. He would have to save himself. Like the resolute salmon, he must journey homeward toward his own headwater, his own birthplace.

He would become a salmon.

Qulen

(Ten)

After many days, the longboats returned with all the hunters except the young husband. The young wife frantically searched the faces of the returning men, asking about her husband. One of the older men spoke to her.

'Your husband is gone,' he said gravely. 'He harpooned a mighty whale. But the harpoon rope was tangled around his ankle, and the whale dragged him into the sea.'

A small airplane flew low along the shoreline, only slightly faster than stall speed. Jack Evanoff held a pair of binoculars on his lap, lifting them to his eyes whenever something caught his attention. Lee Walsh looked out his side window as he piloted the aircraft, its response at such a slow speed a little more sluggish than he liked. As it had done before, on the way from town the small aircraft followed the mainland coast in a generally eastward direction, its bird-like shadow passing over beaches and the narrow mouths to long bays, which extended far back into the glacial valleys. Once the fuel gauge needle reached the halfway point, Lee turned the plane around and flew along the inside of the islands facing the mainland.

It was the best plan, covering the most likely terrain.

Many times the pilot turned the white, blue-striped Citabria around to get a better look at something on a beach. And every time, as it had been before, the thing that caught their eye turned out to be a bear, a deer, a beached buoy or fuel drum, a pile of dark stones, or a log.

After returning to town, Jack followed Lee into the blue metal-sided building to close his flight plan. Rod Clark, the airport manager who had shared the bad news about the discovery of Seth's baseball cap, was waiting to talk to him.

'I got a call while you were out.'

Jack didn't like where the words were headed. The serious tone was contrary to any possibility of good news.

'The Coast Guard and the State Troopers have called off the search. They say it's been long enough.'

Jack looked at Lee, who was leaning over and scribbling something in the open flight-plan book lying on the counter. Then he looked back at the airport manager.

'Are you sure they're calling it off?' he asked. 'I mean, it hasn't been *that* long.'

Rod took the black book from Lee after he signed off on his form.

'They called about an hour ago. I decided not to radio you. I thought it was best to wait until you returned to hear the news in person.'

'What happens now?' Jack asked, visibly shaken.

Clark's tone remained serious but somewhat softer. 'The government won't continue to look for Seth. I'm afraid you're on your own.'

Lee, who hadn't said a word since he first asked for the black book, spoke.

'I know it's hard, Jack. But you may have to accept that your son is gone.'

Jack hadn't allowed himself to think that. He was convinced that Seth was lost somewhere in the Sound, cold and hungry and frightened, praying that his father would find him. The thought filled his mind so much that he couldn't sleep at night; and when he did doze for an hour or so, exhausted, he had fitful nightmares of Seth screaming his name.

Both men said how sorry they were, offering their condolences.

• • • • •

An hour later, Jack walked into The Salty Dawg, the only bar in town, built near the dock at the edge of the harbor overlooking the many boats so that fishermen could spend their hard-earned wages conveniently. Next door was the Puff Inn, the only bed and breakfast in town. The Dawg was crowded and loud. Friday nights were always busy. Though it was bright outside—the summer sun still high—the inside was windowless and dark, the way most bars are, a place where time doesn't matter, except, of course, for closing time, when the regulars shuffle homeward, exhausted, bleary-eyed, and often broke.

Jack walked up to the bar, leaned close to the bartender, and asked her to turn off the wall-mounted television. She smiled and grabbed the remote. When the screen went black, Jack turned toward the crowd, sitting at tables or standing around the two red, felt-covered pool tables.

'Can I have your attention?' he shouted, trying to catch everyone's notice. 'Excuse me!'

The room quieted down.

'You all know who I am,' he said. 'And you all know my son is missing.'

People facing away turned their chairs toward Jack. He could hear the legs scooting on the wood floor.

'By now you've probably heard that the search has been called off.'

Many heads nodded. Word travels fast. A few of the men exchanged whispers with one another.

Jack took off his baseball cap, wrung it in his hands.

'I want to ask you to keep looking for my son. He might still be out there.'

Anyone who has ever lived in a fishing community understands moments like this, when news of a lost ship arrives with its list of lost souls. Every fisherman knows such a list could contain names of friends and relatives—perhaps even one day his own name.

'You all know I lost my wife last year,' he began.

But Jack couldn't finish his sentence. He stood in the dark bar, trembling, trying to net the fleeting words. He looked down at the dark blue hat in his hands, saw his dead wife's name embroidered in gold. Some of the men looked down at their beers, others at the floor. Some pains are unfathomable, too deep to be plumbed. Jack tried to collect himself enough to speak again. Unable, he turned and walked out the door.

He had said enough. Everyone understood.

Someone once said that the world breaks everyone. Most are stronger in the broken place. Some never heal. Jack worried that if he lost his entire family he would be among those too broken to mend.

He looked out over the harbor, at the gently rocking fishing boats, and then he walked down the long dock, turning toward the slip where the *Erin Elizabeth* was moored. By himself, he untied the ropes and motored slowly to the fueling station, where he filled the tank. The salmon swarming into the Sound were no longer of interest to him. The livelihood they represented didn't matter. He would continue the search on his own, leaving first thing in the morning after gathering provisions.

Nothing else mattered.

After returning the boat to its slip and securing it for the night, Jack Evanoff drove home in his pickup truck and walked upstairs to his son's room and sat on the edge of the bed. The springs squeaked. He looked around at the posters on the wall, at the small trophies and ribbons from Seth's earlier youth. A framed photograph stood on the night stand. In it Seth and his mother were standing on the boat, their arms around each other, laughing, though drenched, their hair wet and flat. Jack remembered that happy day, the picnic on the hill.

A tapping sound caught his attention. He looked out the bedroom window. Just then it began to pour outside, a rain so heavy that its falling on the tin roof was thunderous. It reminded him of the night he last saw his son. Staring out the window, Jack wondered if Seth might still be alive, coping with this storm, somehow. He wondered how long anyone could survive such hardship, let alone a boy. He looked down at the photo in his hands, saddened that he had let so much distance come between them. Tears had fallen on the glass. He wiped them away with his fingertips.

'I'm sorry,' the father whispered to the picture of his son. 'I should never have said the things I said to you. I didn't mean it.'

Qula All'inguq

(Eleven)

The old man shuffled close to the young man and spoke again.
* 'I am the chief of the Squirrel People. You and your broth-*
ers have killed all of my children and grandchildren and now
their skins hang outside your house.'
* Suddenly the young man understood what had happened.*
He looked at the girl and saw that she was indeed very beau-
tiful. He felt ashamed and saddened.

Seth climbed the mountain in the middle of the island to
see where he was. From the summit, the world spread
out in every direction. Seth imagined he could see forever.

  To the south lay the vast emptiness of the Pacific Ocean,
unbroken until the southbound waves crashed against
the northern coasts of New Zealand and Australia; and
even further away, against the Antarctic ice shelves at the
southern end of the world. Westward lay the Aleutian

Chain, pointing its long, bony finger at the bend toward Asia. A mile or so northward across the bay was the mainland, only the first several miles green with trees, brush, or grass. After that, an impenetrable blanket of snow, thousands of feet deep in places, buried the Chugach Mountains. Nothing survived there, not even mosquitoes. And eastward—in the direction of home—island after island jutted up from the sea like stepping stones set across a stream. From where he stood, Seth imagined he could see his small town, more than a hundred miles away.

He wiped sweat from his forehead. It had been hard work climbing to the summit. Tucker ate snow from a nearby patch, protected from the afternoon sun in the shadow of a ridge. When he had finished eating, he lay in the snow panting. Soon after, the two companions began the descent back to the beach.

After they'd scrambled down sideways for a few minutes, almost falling down a field of scree, something caught the boy's eye. He stopped to look. It was a boat traveling slowly along the shoreline, just far enough out to stay in deep water, but far away so that Seth couldn't hear the engine. He judged by its speed that the boat would reach the beach where the tiny salmon creek emptied into the sea in a matter of minutes. The distance between where he stood on the mountain slope and the beach was much too far to close in the short time, no matter how fast he ran. Seth began to shout, cupping his hands around his mouth. Alternately, he waved his arms, hoping that the contrasting motion against the unmovable mountain might catch the eye of someone aboard.

But the boat kept its unwavering course.

Seth scrambled down the slope as fast as he could, careful not to twist an ankle, shouting all the while. When he was only half way down, he stopped to look and listen. From where he stood, squinting, the boat looked like his father's. It was the same color and the same shape. But many of the fishing boats in the Sound were white and blue. From a distance, the pilot houses, the giant spools that held the net, and the booms all looked the same.

The boat passed the place where the stream poured into the sea. In a couple minutes it would be out of sight. Seth ran downhill recklessly, regardless of the peril. The tree line was approaching. Once inside the dense forest he would be unable to see, or be seen. At the last minute, while he could still see the boat before he descended into the trees and brush, Seth stopped to look. And just then, as the boat made a slow turn to head toward the next island, Seth could see the back of the boat. And while it was still much too distant to read the individual words, he could see, just barely, two bright yellow dots on either side of the stern—two yellow flowers on either side of the unreadable name.

It was his father.

He ran crashing through the forest, using his hands to protect his face and eyes from limbs and branches.

By the time he reached the gravelly beach, winded, the boat was gone. Seth couldn't believe his misfortune. If he hadn't climbed the mountain, he might have been standing on the beach when the boat passed.

Standing there now, filled with a desperate and unlikely

hope as grey and weathered as beach stones, Seth remembered something his father, in a comic mood, used to say to him.

'If it weren't for bad luck, you'd have no luck at all.'

He had always laughed at the saying in the past. It wasn't funny this time.

When it was clear the boat was not going to return, Seth trudged toward the streamlet, defeated, pushed along by his empty stomach. Tucker ran ahead, happily chasing shorebirds and seagulls, oblivious to self-doubt, excruciating disappointment, loneliness.

At that moment, Seth wished he were a dog.

Upon reaching the stream, Seth saw a salmon stranded in a small pool left behind when the tide went out. It was a simple matter to catch it. Luckily, the bears were nowhere in sight. After gutting the fish with his pocketknife, Seth tried to make a fire again. Although he was growing accustomed to eating his food raw, he wanted to roast the fish over a fire. He gathered tinder and dry wood, stopping every so often to shout at Tucker, who kept sneaking up to lick the salmon.

But try as he might, with the determination of an athlete, no sparks arose from his futile attempts with stick or stone. He kept at it for a long time, his frustration building. Without matches or a lighter he would have to eat the fish raw. Seth tossed the useless sticks aside and picked a handful of dandelions growing above the hide tide line. He knew they were edible. His mother sometimes made dandelion salad.

While the slant sun watched as Seth and Tucker ate

their supper of fish and weed, two curious seals swam close to shore, their sleek heads bobbing on the sparkling surface of the sea. Seth cut two chunks of tail meat and tossed them at the seals, which raced for the pieces, beating the hovering seagulls.

Seth remembered his grandmother's story of how the first seals came into existence. She had told it to him when they were standing on the dock watching some seals swimming amid the moored boats. Seals frequent harbors, catching salmon that inadvertently fall overboard during unloading or eating discarded halibut after they are filleted, their corpses tossed into the water.

It was a strange myth as myths go, unsettling even.

Sitting on a boulder eating his supper of salmon and dandelions in the sunshine, sharing the fish with Tucker, who, to his credit, sat patiently waiting for his next bite, Seth recited the story to himself, his memory stumbling at times to remember the details. Even in his mind, he began the story the way all such stories begin.

A long time ago.

As young as he was, Seth vaguely understood the reason. To begin a story in the long ago, in deep time—dateless and immeasurable—guards its usefulness, even its veracity. Stories set in a known history, in a known place and time, as are legends, are easily cut up, like canned salmon, every part questioned, their full purpose ruined. All important stories, no matter where they arise in the world or in what language, begin in a similar manner—time out of time, being out of being—existing only to exist, for no sake, for every sake. There can be meaningful truths in myths that do not depend on fact. The power of myths does not require steadfast belief in the story: that is the realm of religion.

In his own way, Seth knew these things.

And so he began.

A long time ago there was a girl who lived in a small village. The day came when she was old enough to marry. One night, a man crept into her room and forced himself on her. It was so dark she couldn't see who the man was. The next night, he came again, and the night after that. But she was smart, that girl. The next time the man stole into her room, she scratched his face with her fingernails. The next morning, she walked around the village, looking for a man with scratches on his face. She found him. To her horror, she saw that he was her own brother! Ashamed, she ran to the cliff at the edge of the village and hurled herself into the sea. But instead of drowning, she surfaced as a seal! She had turned into the very first female seal. Seeing what his dishonored sister had done and unable to live with his own shame, the brother also cast himself off the cliff. And he surfaced also as the first male seal.

The end of that story had always bothered Seth. How had anything changed for the poor girl except her appearance? He remembered the sound of his grandmother's voice as she told him the story. Why couldn't her myths be more like fairy tales? Unlike fairy tales, which begin cruelly and are frightening but generally end happily, myths rarely have joyful endings. But then he thought, how can they? The world is a hard, breaking place.

There must be equally hard stories.

And then Seth also remembered his grandmother's story

of how an entire village was once destroyed by a volcano after some irreverent boys cast stones at salmon spawning in a stream. No second chances in that story. Nature rarely gives a break.

Sitting there with his hands dripping in raw fish flesh and slime, Seth understood that some stories are about how ruthless and unforgiving life is, and that they are that way to help us navigate through rough seas. Perhaps he himself would one day be a myth, the story of a boy and his faithful dog lost at sea. It would be the myth that would survive, even if he did not.

After supper, Seth and Tucker walked along the beach. Two deer stepped out from the brush far ahead of them, stopped to look, wearily, lifting one front leg then the other, ready to flee in an instant, their ears and white tail twitching. Tucker saw them. He barked, and the nervous deer bounded back into the forest.

Seth stood at the edge of the sea facing the mainland, measuring the watery distance between.

A mile, he thought. *It was about a mile to the other side.*

Qula Atel'ek

(Twelve)

'We did not know that you live like people,' the young man replied shamefully, tears filling the wells of his eyes. 'We did not know that you love your children and grandchildren. I am sorry. Forgive me. I will tell my brothers not to hunt your people any longer.'

Seth combed the beach for rope. He found several pieces of varying lengths and colors. He was surprised how much rope was washed ashore, undoubtedly from snagged and lost fishing nets. Combining these newly found pieces of rope with those he had found earlier and used to hold his shelter together, he lashed three grey driftwood logs into a makeshift raft. It was more awkward-looking canoe than square platform, like the one he imagined Huck Finn and the slave Jim fashioned to float the Mississippi, the one chewed up by the paddle-wheeler. He would use it to cross to the mainland, a distance far too great to swim, especially since tidal surges poured only between the islands like a river, not toward the mainland.

Seth even found a piece of lumber that would serve as a paddle.

But most important, he found a one-liter plastic soda bottle with an inch of flat cola still inside. It was a necessary find. Seth had no idea how often he would find fresh drinking water once he left the island. With the capped bottle, he could at least carry some water with him wherever he went until he found another source. He rinsed and filled it in the stream and tied a piece of cord from a frayed rope around the neck so he could sling it over his shoulder like a canteen.

While he worked, building his means of escape at the edge of the high-tide line, a chilling breeze swept across the sea. Luckily, the yellow raincoat offered some protection from the wind's teeth. Frequently, Seth had to stop to pull up his jeans, which had become loose on him. Eventually, he tightened his belt to keep them from falling down.

When he was finished securing his canoe-raft, he and Tucker waited for the slack tide, the interval between tidal shifts when the tide is neither coming nor going, neither rising nor falling, that window of opportunity when the sea is nearly as unmoving as a lake. When the moment arrived, Seth dragged the craft into the water and climbed aboard, careful not to flip it over. Two feet wide, more or less, the raft was unstable and tipsy. But with only enough rope to lash the three logs, he could not have built it wider.

Straddling the raft with his legs dangling in the water

on either side, Seth motioned for Tucker to join him. It took some trial and error, but eventually he encouraged the dog to lie down and remain still. Using the impromptu paddle, Seth turned the bow toward the mainland and struck deep into the water ahead of him, pulling hard and long on one side and then the other, making each stroke count, the way his father had taught him. With the island now at his back, the uncertain craft glided landward.

A sea otter accompanied him for a while.

A little more than halfway across, Seth noticed that the raft was sitting lower in the water. The grey beach logs were partially waterlogged from each high tide that had reached them. Once in the sea, they absorbed even more water, sponge-like, gaining weight, losing buoyancy. The craft was sinking. Seth paddled faster, racing against the inevitable. A few minutes later, the water was up to his waist. Tucker stood looking nervously at his submerged paws, as if he were deciding whether to go down with the ship or jump overboard and swim for it.

Every dog for himself.

By the time they were close to the mainland beach, the raft had sunk from beneath them, and Seth and Tucker had to swim for shore. Almost humorously, like a bad joke, Seth thought about his iPod as he swam behind Tucker.

'How could it possibly ever work again?' he thought and laughed to himself.

The two castaways sat on the beach for a while, letting the sun warm and dry them, while the tide slowly retreated, shrinking the bay. Toward evening, they walked along the narrow beach with the sun at their back. Once the tide

John Smelcer

returned, the going was made difficult by the thick vegetation through which the rising water forced them to walk above the high-tide line. At times Seth and Tucker had to force their way through nearly impenetrable brush and over rocky outcrops.

They spent the hungry night sleeping on the grassy ledge of a rocky outcrop a dozen feet above the lapping sea, boy and dog dreaming of food, urged on by their complaining stomachs, as empty as a shallow bay at low tide.

The next morning, after hiking for a couple miles and passing a washed up and decayed beluga whale—infested with flies and maggots—the two travelers stopped at a safe distance from a sow brown bear with two-year-old cubs digging in the dark sand and mud, rooting in the holes with their snouts. From time to time they'd pull up a long golden-brown colored clam with their teeth, expertly pry it open with their claws, and consume the slimy meat inside. Even from a considerable distance, Seth could see that they were razor clams, so named because of their brittle, razor-thin shells, which live only in muddy and sandy, not gravel, beaches like the beaches most common in the Sound. He and his parents had often gone clam digging. He loved it. It was so messy, but so much fun finding the little holes in the mucky sand and then digging for the clams on the seaward side of the holes. When they finished their searching and gathering, retreating from the advancing tide, the beach always looked the way this beach did, with dozens of craters, as if a bomber had dropped its payload on the sandy shore.

Seth and Tucker circled up through the thick and tangled

woods, moving far down the beach, giving ample space between themselves and the bears. Using a flat rock, Seth dug after the buried clams, stopping occasionally to keep an eye on the bears. The stone worked so well as a hand shovel that pretty soon Seth had caught half a dozen clams, some as long as ten inches. Each time Seth pulled one out from a hole, Tucker jumped at the chance to continue digging in the same place, certain of more clams.

He never learned and he never found one.

When he had harvested ten fat clams, Seth used his pocket knife to open each one. Unlike steamer clams, razor clams open easily once slit down the middle. Seth would open and eat two, then open a clam for Tucker. Before long, both boy and dog had eaten their fill of the raw, slimy meat. Seth liked the taste of the clams far better than he did the black mussels, and grimaced and gagged less.

Tucker didn't seem to care one way or the other.

A raven flew down and pecked at the little bits of meat and guts left in the shells.

After their meal, Seth turned his attention back to the matter of getting home. He knew that his town was the first fishing community along the coast toward the east. If he followed the coastline, he'd eventually run into it, though he had no idea exactly how far away that might be. He knew, too, that to go inland was suicide. He remembered the view from the mountain top, how mountain after mountain loomed in the great distance, buried almost to their spiky peaks under snow, the accumulation of ten thousand years or longer.

Only death lived there.

No, thought Seth, to follow the coast was the surest bet. With his plan formulated, he and Tucker set off in the direction of home, their strength and determination bolstered by their satisfied bellies.

After about an hour's hike, the shore abruptly turned inland, to the north, following a long, narrow bay that was flanked by green mountains on both sides. From where he stood, Seth could see the other side less than a quarter of a mile away. If it weren't for the water, they could walk across in about five minutes. He could almost throw a rock that far, he mused, though he knew he really couldn't.

For the next two days the boy and his dog worked their way along and around the narrow bay, the going made slow by dense brush, steep cliffs, and changing tides. After two full days, exhausted, they stood across from the exact same point where they had begun, with less than a quarter mile of water between. Seth couldn't believe they had traveled so far—fifteen to twenty miles he estimated—only to end up right back at the mouth of the bay.

Standing there, looking backward toward their recent past, defeated, it dawned on Seth that the entire coast of the Sound was like this, beset by dozens and dozens of similar bays, many with their northern terminus guarded by untraversable glaciers. He recalled having seen with his own eyes such glacially bound bays the few times he and his parents had flown to Anchorage. To follow the coast-line was impossible.

The only way home was by using the islands in the sea.

Qula Pinga'an

(Thirteen)

But the chief was still sad. 'It is too late to stop killing us,' he said. 'We are all dead now. My granddaughter and I are all that is left of our people.'

'I did not mean to kill you all,' exclaimed the young hunter with tears filling his eyes. 'Isn't there something I can do?'

'There is a way,' replied the old chief. 'I can make you a great shaman and you can return my people.'

Seth found a driftwood log. He could tell by its weight that it was drier than the logs he had used to fashion the raft. He dragged it down to the beach from well above the high-tide line. When the currents were right, the flow of surging tide going toward the easterly island, he pushed the log into the water and wrapped an arm around it, using his free arm to paddle. Tucker swam alongside. Whenever the dog appeared to grow tired, Seth placed his arm around his upper chest, lifting Tucker's head above water. In such a manner, they eventually found their way to the beach.

Seth recognized the island.

His father had anchored here many times to picnic, telling the story of what happened to the people who used to live in this place. It was one of the most tragic, little-known stories of Alaskan history, of American history.

His father said that a village used to exist at the exact place where Seth now stood on the beach, looking out over the sparkling water at a raft of floating ducks. More than a hundred people had lived here in small houses. There had been a church, a cemetery, a long dock, a village store, even a schoolhouse. Seth could see the remains of the dilapidated schoolhouse on the top of the hill overlooking the beach, its roof caved in, a stark reminder of what had happened here.

Seth remembered the story the way his father had told him.

In March of 1964, barely five years after Alaska became the forty-ninth state, the largest earthquake ever recorded in North America rocked south-central Alaska.

It was Good Friday. The epicenter of the quake was offshore, deep in the earth beneath Prince William Sound. The quake destroyed parts of Anchorage, Seward, and Valdez, collapsing roads, streets, and buildings. While most Alaskans are aware of the effects of the quake on the mostly white towns, almost no one knows the untold story of Chenega, the small Native village that used to stand along this shore.

A side effect of the earthquake was the creation of four giant tidal waves, called tsunamis, which formed offshore near the epicenter. The waves, each as tall as a six-storey building, raced across the Sound at speeds over 300 miles per hour, aimed right at the tiny, unsuspecting village.

Seth was always astonished that waves could travel so fast. It was hard to imagine.

Without warning, the waves blasted through everything like giant bulldozers made of churning seawater and sea-bottom debris, destroying whatever was in their path, buildings and people alike. The fortunate ran uphill as fast as they could. The next day there was nothing left of the village, not even the lumber from the shattered houses and boat hulls and timbers from the dock.

Nothing floated in the bay. The tides had carried it all away, erasing the community from the face of the earth. All they found was the Bible from the church, preserved in a new church to this day.

Twenty-six people, more than a quarter of the village population, died that day.

Seth looked behind him at where the village used to be. He marveled at how far up the hill the waves must have traveled. Only the old schoolhouse perched at the top of the hill survived untouched. Now time was claiming even that.

Seth walked up to the schoolhouse and found a plaque with the names of the dead. He read them all, one after the other, recognizing some of the family names from his own town.

• • • • •

Seth and Tucker stayed on the island for several days, eating whatever the island provided, which wasn't much. The villagers who had lived there used boats to catch salmon and hunt seals. One of the strangest things the castaways ate was gumboots. Seth knew that 'gumboots' was not their real name but what his father called a form of chiton, a sea slug in a hard shell that clings to rocks like barnacles, easily harvested at low tide.

Alaska's *escargot*.

Seth pried them off boulders with his knife, and, like always, he and Tucker ate them raw. He didn't know why they were called gumboots, perhaps because they are so rubbery, like eating boiled shoe leather. Seth even remembered the Alutiiq word his grandmother had taught him: *uuqiituk*. He liked saying that word, the way his mouth moved when making the unfamiliar sounds: oo-KEE-duk. He remembered that some famous British writer had once said that the most beautiful word in the English language is *cellar door*.

He'd obviously never heard Alutiiq.

While Seth ate the slimy snails, swallowing them instead of chewing them, wishing he were eating donuts instead.

Many times Seth tried to make a fire—unsuccessfully. And twice, different fishing boats passed the island too far away for anyone aboard to see the boy waving from shore. A smoke signal could have ended his journey on either occasion. But it wasn't to be. Without fire, Seth and Tucker were all but invisible to the passing world. Only their own muscles and ingenuity and perseverance would rescue them.

One afternoon, Seth found a bush full of small, white berries. While it was still too early in the summer for blueberries or cranberries or rosehips, these looked ready to eat. Seth ate a few. They tasted bitter. But he knew that berries contain important nutrients, like Vitamin C to reduce scurvy, old-time sailors' bane, so he swallowed them nonetheless. He gave some to Tucker as well. The dog ate a few, but didn't seem to like them very much and turned his nose away.

After Seth had eaten several handfuls, the two castaways explored the low tide pools, looking for food. While they were walking along the beach, Tucker suddenly stopped and retched, throwing up the berries. He vomited several times, until nothing came up any longer but slick bile. All the while, Seth squatted beside him, patting the dog's back, encouraging him the way his mother sometimes did whenever he had been sick.

'It's OK, boy. You'll be all right.'

A little further down the beach, Seth suddenly felt a wave of nausea that stopped him in his tracks. His face broke into a sweat, and he dropped to his knees, weak and dizzy. And then it came. He began to throw up like Tucker, violently. The hot, sour vomit even came up through his nose. He hated the dry heaves most, when nothing came up at all, yet the sickened stomach still tried to purge itself. The heaves were so forceful that Seth was sure he would retch up his lung or part of his stomach.

Weakened and exhausted, his gut muscles as sore as if he had done a thousand sit-ups, Seth climbed up above the high tide line and lay down in some tall grass. Tucker lay down and looked listlessly at his young master, the rim of his eyes red and sagging. Seth felt the dog's nose. It was warm. He remembered his parents telling him that a warm nose means a dog is sick. He didn't need a warm nose to know that.

The vomiting was a dead giveaway.

For the next twenty-four hours, the two of them lay in the grass, hidden from seagulls and any passing boats. Seth's cold sweats continued on and off, his clothes drenched, his muscles tight and trembling. Several times he had to raise himself to his knees to heave. He'd collapse afterwards, too weak to hold himself up for long, too weak to swat away mosquitoes. At one point, dreamlike, Seth thought he heard a boat engine and voices close by, but he was too weak to pull himself up to look.

While he lay curled beside his dog, Seth thought about his life since his mother had died, how he spent all his time sitting in his room, pretty much ignoring his friends, watching television, listening to his music, playing video games, surfing the internet, conversing in chat rooms, and texting on his mobile phone instead of spending time with real human beings. He saw himself sitting all alone in his small room while his friends played football and basketball, went swimming, had sleepovers, or just hung around the pizzeria in town.

Looking at himself that way, distantly, Seth felt a change taking place, something he could actually feel above the continuing waves of nausea. He felt disconnected, unleashed from all those solitary moments and moods, the inward diversions from the outside world. He suddenly felt no connection at all to those things he had overused to isolate himself from everyone. And just as suddenly, Seth missed and longed for his father.

He thought about what his father had gone through on the day of the wreck, the accident that killed his mother, how his father must have felt as he crawled over to his wife, saw her lying broken in the snow, unable to save her, the winter cold and darkness absorbing her warmth and light.

Seth began to cry.

For the first time—really for the very first time—he felt his father's loss, the grief that must lie beneath his facade of strength and stoicism, which Seth had always viewed as a lack of caring, or worse, as indifference. He cried harder, not just for himself and the loss of his mother, but for his father, for his loss—of his wife and, now, of his son.

That night, as he lay shivering in a sweaty delirium, Seth dreamed that he was grown, a shabby figure like Robinson Crusoe climbing palm trees to cut coconuts, marking days with scratches on a tree. The dream disturbed Seth, the notion of being lost for so many years. He mumbled in his sleep, occasionally calling out, waking Tucker. He also had a strange dream in which the dead people of the island, children and adults alike, came and danced around him. His mother was there, too. In the vision, he danced with the ghosts, the sound of seal skin drums echoing across the sea.

It was the first time Seth had dreamed of his mother since her death.

By late afternoon the next day, Seth was feeling strong enough to get up and look for food and fresh water. Both boy and dog were dehydrated from their ordeal. As they walked along the beach in search of food for their very empty stomachs, Seth had to stop to tighten his belt one more hole to keep his jeans from falling down. The knees were almost worn out, the hems frayed. He was shedding pounds the way mountains shed snow in the spring and summer—a trickle at first, then faster and faster, the alpine snow fields shrinking to nothingness. His belt was running out of holes.

Tucker looked leaner as well—his ribs beginning to show—but his coat was still shiny, the sign of a healthy dog.

Seth's weight wasn't the only thing changing. As he knelt over a pool of rainwater quenching his thirst, he saw the reflection of his thinning face covered with a scruffy beard and sideburns, his dark hair disheveled.

Everything about him was changing.

Qula Staaman

(Fourteen)

The young woman didn't believe that her husband was dead. She climbed a steep hill at the edge of the sea and stood watching for him. For weeks, her mother and sisters brought her food and drink. One day, after months, the comforters returned and found only a pile of stones where she had stood.

M orning, Jack!' Lucky shouted up from the dock.

Jack came out from the pilothouse wearing a white T-shirt, a cup of coffee in his hand.

'Morning,' he replied. 'Got time for a cup of coffee?'

'Always got time for a friend.'

Lucky climbed aboard and followed Jack into the galley, helping himself to a cup. He knew which cabinet they were in. He joined Jack, who removed his dark blue cap when they sat down at the small table.

'How's things?' Jack asked.

'Been fishing with Joe Weil on the *Luck of the Irish*,' said Lucky, stirring a spoon of sugar into his cup.

'I heard. How's that working out?'

Lucky looked down as he spoke, as if he were ashamed of himself, which he was in a way for abandoning his long-time captain.

'The season's shaping up pretty good so far. Not as good as last year, though.'

Neither spoke for a couple of minutes. Lucky was the first to break the silence.

'I see you still have the dog's stuff,' he said, looking at the food dish on the floor.

Jack turned to look at it, stared at it for a moment, as though he hadn't seen it before, as if he didn't know what it was.

'Guess I just forgot to get rid of it,' he said finally.

'You know, Jack, you have to let go sometime and move on with your life.'

'It's just a bowl,' Jack growled.

'Yeah, it's just a bowl, but it's like the other things you haven't let go of.'

'Like what?' asked Jack, leaning back and crossing his arms over his chest.

'Like that video game sitting on the counter. Why do you keep it?'

'I don't know,' answered Jack. 'It's not hurting anything to sit over there.'

'But it's not doing any good, either . . . just reminding you of your son.'

Both men were quiet again.

'I gotta go,' said Lucky, finishing his coffee and setting it in the small galley sink. 'We're heading out. But I need to say something, Jack, and you gotta listen. Bad things happen. No one can control it. But you got to keep going in spite of it, maybe *because* of it.'

'What are you trying to say, Lucky, that I should just forget my family?'

Lucky pushed his chair under the table, stood behind it, a barrier for his guilt.

'No one's saying that, Jack. But if you don't get back to fishing, you're going to lose everything: your house, your boat, your livelihood. What's happened to you shouldn't have happened to anyone. No one's blaming you for being sad. But you can't give up. What does that say to the rest of us?'

Lucky stood in the doorway for a moment, letting his words sink into the depths of his friend's darkness, and then he turned and left.

Jack sat at the table for a long time, slowly turning his empty cup, staring out the window. Finally, he stood up and put his baseball cap back on.

'He's wrong. It hasn't been that long.'

• • • • •

Jack knew that Lucky was right in some ways. He *had* spent all of his time looking for his son, which meant he wasn't making money fishing. That's why Lucky wouldn't go out with him anymore. He had to make a living. At the rate he was going, Jack wouldn't be able to pay the loan on his boat, which meant he really could lose his livelihood and his only means of searching for Seth. Besides, diesel was expensive. He had to pay for it somehow.

Jack drove up to the town's cemetery on a hill overlooking the bay. He sat in the quiet truck for a long time. Then he climbed out, slammed the squeaky door, and gathered wild flowers from alongside the gravel parking lot, mostly dandelions, fireweed, and forget-me-nots, Alaska's state flower. The yellow, pink, and blue bouquet looked lovely to Jack. He laid it on the ground beside his wife's gravestone, which was simply engraved with two small words.

Wife. Mother.

He knelt on the grass, saying nothing, running a hand along the smooth surface of the stone, his fingers tracing the groove of the words. Several times he looked high into the sky, saying nothing, the drifting clouds saying even less.

Finally, he stood up and straightened himself.

'I'll find our boy. I promise.'

Jack drove straight home and pulled his wife's car out from the garage, where it had been parked since the day before she died. He washed and cleaned it and sold it to the only used car dealer in town. The man knew why Jack was selling it, so he gave him more than it was worth.

Sometimes compassion comes from the most unlikely places.

Jack took part of the money and paid his boat loan for several months. Then he walked down to the marina and put some money on account at the fuel depot. Afterwards, he felt better than he thought he would. Somehow, selling his wife's car helped. In his mind, it seemed as if she were contributing to the search for their son.

Later that evening, under a blue, cloudless sky, the *Erin Elizabeth* cleared the harbor, turned its bow westward, and headed into the blinding sun, followed by a flock of noisy seagulls.

Qula Talliman

(Fifteen)

The remorseful young man agreed, and so the old man began to work his powerful magic. He took the hunter outside and tied his limbs to the Great Tree. Then he pushed sharp needles made of bone with string made of gut through the young man's skin and pulled them tight in every direction, tying the ends of the strings to the tree's branches.

There was a piercing needle for every dead squirrel.

Two pink buoys bobbed against a rocky shore.

Seth waded out to retrieve them. Tucker stared curiously from the rocks, wondering if the strange floating objects were something to eat. Giant apples, perhaps. Each buoy was as big as a beach ball. Seth recognized what they were used for. Net floats. His father used them on his boat to float net lines and for marking submerged crab pots—resting on the bottom of the sea, tethered by long ropes. Although deep red when new, the color of the rubber quickly fades to pink from sunlight and the weather. The bottom of the buoys with their eyelets were still a deep blue. From where he stood, Seth could see they were connected by a long rope.

As Seth waded ashore with his catch, an idea was forming in his mind. He cut one end of the long rope, shortening it to a little less than three feet. Then he retied it, making sure the knots securing it to the buoys were tight. Now, he could use his double-buoy invention as a kind of unsinkable life preserver.

When the tide was just right, Seth waded into the bay and situated himself so that the short rope ran across his chest and under each armpit. The buoys floating on either side reminded him of the armbands his mother strapped around his little body when he was first learning to swim. In such a fashion, he was able to use his arms to swim while floating effortlessly.

He turned and called Tucker, who splashed into the water and swam around him in an eager circle. Together, they struck out toward the next eastward island. Whenever Tucker grew tired, Seth held him close, holding his head well above the water, their combined weight barely affecting the two, stout buoys.

Without incident, the two made it ashore to a small island, a landmass as tiny as their first landfall the night they fell overboard. Although Seth and Tucker were cold from their swim, the sun quickly warmed them. By midday, followed by his dog, Seth used his flotation device to swim to the next, much larger island, leaving behind the provisionless pit stop on their journey.

They were making good headway, the miles falling away.

Come mid-afternoon, Seth explored their new home looking for something to eat. Island hopping burned calories.

During his search he made his way into a small cove with a fast-flowing creek pouring into the far end. The water at the mouth of the stream was choked with salmon, hundreds of them, perhaps thousands. There were so many fish that the light-grey pebbly bottom of the cove was obscured by salmon. The place was a fisherman's dream. If Seth only had a fishing rod he could catch as many fish as he needed. Without one, though, it would be almost impossible to catch one. Every time he waded into the water to snatch one, the cove's surface would roil with splashing and darting fish, some as long as his leg.

As he stood knee-deep trying to figure out how to catch his supper, Seth remembered the word for salmon his grandmother had taught him.

Igalluk.

She had made her grandson say the word many times until he pronounced it correctly.

Ee-GOL-luk.

Afterwards, she told him that there was an Alutiiq name for each of the five salmon species: reds, silvers, pinks, kings, and chums. Most Alaskans call chums 'dog salmon' because in the old days the chums, the least tasty of the five species, were dried and stored to feed their dog sled team all winter.

Seth couldn't remember all the names, but he remembered *igalluk.*

The memory of his grandmother teaching him that day saddened him. She passed away only a month later. Seth remembered what she had demanded of him the day she died.

'Don't turn away from your heritage the way your father did. Promise me, grandson, that you will not forget the things I have taught you.'

Seth kissed her forehead and promised. What else could he say at a moment like that, a moment chiseled in stone, everlasting in memory?

'I promise, Umma,' he'd told her, using the Alutiiq word for grandmother.

She'd slipped away after that, quietly and peacefully, surrounded by her children and grandchildren.

Standing there in the shallows of the cove, watching the darting salmon beyond his grasp, Seth suddenly had an idea. He knew how he might catch a salmon. He rummaged along the shore looking for a suitably long pole-like branch. When he found one, he sharpened the end with his pocketknife. Then he waded into the water behind the fish, slowly working his way toward the shallow, narrow stream. From behind, his shadow didn't fall on the large school, frightening them. When he was close enough, he stabbed a fish, not throwing the spear. The sharp point penetrated all the way through, but the flapping, wiggling fish slipped off and swam away, most likely to die later from its wound. Seth tried twice more, and both times his supper escaped.

The losses frustrated Seth. Tucker had an expression that seemed to say, 'So, where's supper? Look at them all. What's so hard? Just get one. What's up with the stick?'

Seth sat down on the beach and thought about his technique. It dawned on him that he needed something on the spear tip to keep the fish from sliding off once stabbed. He used the point of his knife to cut a small slot through the spear, just a few inches above the sharpened tip. Then, he found and cut a slender branch from a shrub, skinny enough to fit through the slot. He cut off both ends until only a couple of inches protruded from either side. The green branch was slightly flexible. Seth hoped the addition to his spear would act as a barb, securing the salmon long enough to seize it.

Armed with his invention, Seth waded into the water again, and this time when he speared a salmon, it was unable to slide off the end and escape. In no time, the proud, young fisherman had caught two fish, a meal fit for a king. Seth gutted both, and after he and Tucker had consumed one raw (as always), he tied the other to a piece of rope and kept it fresh in the water.

While looking at the skein full of bright-red salmon eggs he had pulled out from both fish and discarded when he gutted them, Seth decided to try preparing something he recalled from his grandmother, something she and other elders liked to eat. He built a little circle of rocks near the edge of the creek and placed the eggs inside, so that they were chilled by the water, but the stone structure kept them from being washed away. He covered the stone circle with leafy branches so that hovering seagulls wouldn't see them and eat them all. By the next morning, the eggs would turn from bright red to a pale pink. The exposure to the fresh water would make them somewhat hard.

Seth recalled how the elders referred to this delicacy as *beebles*. He remembered the word because it sounded so funny. His grandmother used to say it over and over and then laugh. She said that no one knew for sure where the word came from. It's not a Native word. Seth decided, when he first ate them, that they must have got that funny name because they looked and felt like tiny pink bee-bees. Though oily and fishy-tasting, they were very nutritious, making popping sounds when you chewed them.

After a long and restless night, fearful of bears because of the salmon-plentiful creek, Seth and Tucker ate the *beebles* for breakfast.

While they ate, a distant rumbling caught their attention. A jet airliner was flying over thirty thousand feet above them, its long white contrail dissolving in its path. Seth didn't even move. There was no need. From such a height, the airplane was of no help to them whatsoever. Even if he somehow managed a signal fire, no one aboard an airliner five or six miles above would notice.

Later that day, a storm blew in from the gulf. It was almost as bad as the one that launched their adventure. The slant, wind-driven rain lashed at everything, tamping down the earth itself. The little stream swelled and turned muddy, and the salmon went out to sea. In no time, the mossy forest was rain sodden. Tree branches provided little protection. Seth wandered the island seeking shelter from the storm with Tucker trailing behind him, a drenched and pathetic orange mop with four legs.

Seth eventually discovered a cave in the side of a hill, its mouth partially concealed by undergrowth. He crawled inside. Immediately, the cavern opened up, revealing a large room, tall enough to stand in. Grey light filtered down from several holes in the ceiling. But it was mostly dry. It took a moment for Seth's eyes to adjust to the near darkness.

The room, for lack of a better word, was about twenty or thirty feet wide, and maybe twice as deep, the roof of the cave slanting lower toward the far back wall. It wasn't your traditional cave with stalactites and stalagmites. Large rocks were strewn on the floor where they had fallen from the ceiling.

As Seth made his way around the cave, something snapped underfoot. It sounded like a branch or twig. He bent down to see what it was. To his horror he saw that it was a skeleton. A human skeleton. He jumped back. As his eyes focused, he saw that there were two others nearby. After the initial fear subsided, Seth examined the bones more closely. He found a sword lying near one with some kind of markings. He carried it near the entrance where the light was better. The markings near the hilt of the sword looked like writing he had seen in a Japanese restaurant his mother used to make his father take them to a couple times a year. Although Seth didn't read or speak Japanese, he recognized the shape of the characters. Besides, he knew that it wasn't German, French, or Spanish, classes offered at school. A few minutes later he found an old, rusted pistol with some markings that looked similar. The slide and magazine wouldn't move, welded shut by decades of rust.

But what astonished Seth the most was what he eventually noticed on the wall toward the rear of the cave. Someone had scratched symbols into the stone, most likely with the point of the sword. There were three short vertical sets of symbols. Wondering what the three brief columns of strange figures might mean, he realized that there were three skeletons and the scratchings were probably their names.

While he sat on a rock in the cave waiting for the storm to subside, Seth puzzled over his gruesome discovery. How had the three Japanese ended up inside the cave? And how long had they been here?

He remembered from his Alaska history class how Japan had attacked Alaska during World War II. Everyone knows about Pearl Harbor in Hawaii, but the Alaskan invasion remains largely forgotten. The battles were far away on two tiny islands at the western end of the Aleutian chain, a thin arm of islands that extends over a thousand miles toward Asia—and Japan. Seth remembered that the battles raged all winter on tiny Kiska and Attu. The winter was hard on both sides, especially on the American soldiers, who had been diverted to Alaska after training for desert warfare in Africa. They arrived without proper clothing and equipment for the frigid, hostile conditions.

Frostbite took its toll.

Many American soldiers suffered amputated fingers and toes.

But the soldiers on both sides weren't the only ones to suffer. The local Natives, called Aleuts, suffered almost as much, perhaps even more. The American government, worried that the invasion might spread to the rest of the islands, evacuated the Natives. They forcibly removed them from their homes and shipped them to a dilapidated old fishing cannery a thousand miles away. It seemed like no one from the government even bothered to investigate the site or its structures, which had broken windows, leaky roofs, and no heat source or running water or latrines. They dropped off the Aleuts and left them, largely forgotten, until the end of the war. They said it was for their own protection. It bothered Seth that the Aleuts, citizens of Alaska, a territory of the United States, were treated worse than the Japanese prisoners.

Today, the internment place is littered with untended graves.

At the very end of the Aleutian Island battle, just as an armada of American transport ships arrived through a thick fog carrying reinforcements, several small, two-man Japanese reconnaissance submarines escaped the makeshift harbor. Each had enough diesel fuel to keep their engines running for maybe a thousand miles.

Seth remembered reading that none of the little submarines were ever captured.

Looking at the skeletons and the words cut into the wall, Seth imagined that these three men might have crammed themselves into one of those tiny subs and made their way up the Aleutian Chain until running out of fuel. Perhaps they made their way toward the mainland just as he and Tucker were trying to do. They must have survived off the land until their deaths—from cold, from exposure, from hunger. Apparently, just before they died, they carved their names into the wall, in the event that they were ever discovered, and maybe a short message elsewhere in the cave that Seth had failed to notice.

Perhaps the last one alive was assigned the morbid task.

Seth calculated that the bodies must have lain here in the dank, grey darkness for almost seventy years.

The idea of dying alone on one of hundreds of uninhabited islands hit home with Seth. If it had taken so long for him to blindly stumble upon this cave, how long might it be until someone found his body—if ever? He hated the cave for what it represented—a secret mausoleum. He crept to the entrance and sat with his back against the moist wall, sprinkled by rain, petting Tucker, breathing in fresh air, bathed in dim light, waiting for the storm to pass.

There was no way he would spend the night inside the cave with its musty smell of death.

Qula Arwinlen

(Sixteen)

The young man screamed in pain, but the old man said the pain was part of the power. When the chief was finished, he left the Indian hanging for three days. On the third day he returned and sang a magic song for three more days. He did not rest, nor did he eat or sleep. After that, he left the young hunter alone.

Eventually, the storm passed, and the islands passed, day after day, week after week. But Seth's mind was always on home, always on his father. By now, autumn had arrived in Alaska, and with it arrived the birds, countless millions of them heading south for the winter. The skies and bays were full of noisy birds.

Autumn dragged darkness in its wake.

The days grew shorter and colder, and stars filled the night sky. Autumn is so brief in the Far North that locals call it *fell*, because one day the leaves are on the trees and the next day they are not. But with the cold mornings and nights came some good news. The bothersome mosquitoes became active only during the warmest part of the day, and ripe berries were everywhere. Seth and Tucker gorged on blueberries, cranberries, wild raspberries, and even rosehips. Consuming so many berries was a great relief from raw fish and clams and mussels, but the new diet also caused the digestive systems of both boy and dog to ring alarm bells. Seth found himself squatting in the bushes as often as Tucker.

One morning, while walking along a beach in search of food and drinking water, Seth found a large piece of green canvas tangled in some bushes. He dragged it out, shook it, and laid it flat on the ground. It was in good shape. He used his pocketknife to cut a square about four feet or five across with a sizable hole in the middle for his head and two smaller holes for his arms. It looked like a poncho. He pulled it over his head, pushed his arms through their holes, and secured the canvas over his slicker with a length of rope tied around his waist. He slung the plastic soda bottle canteen over his shoulder. His appearance reminded him of a character in an action movie. By now, Seth had run out of holes on his leather belt, and he had punched three more holes to keep his jeans up.

He used what remained of the canvas as a blanket for himself and Tucker.

And although the canvas kept them a little warmer at night, Seth worried about the future. As winter approached and finally settled in, burying the islands of the Sound in deep, impenetrable snow, the canvas would not be enough to protect them. Without fire, he and Tucker wouldn't last long. Besides, there would be little to eat in winter, and the sea would be far too cold for swimming.

But for now, winter was weeks away, and home was closer than ever. While Seth had no idea precisely how far away, he knew that he was near the place where the *Exxon Valdez* wrecked, spilling its cargo of crude oil. That meant he was closing in on justifiable hope. Besides, giant oil tankers, a thousand feet long, regularly navigated these channels. Someone aboard one of them was bound to see them.

It was only a matter of time.

A thick bank of fog rolled into the Sound, its long, grey fingers clutching mountain peaks and crags as if to hold itself from blowing away. The fog was so dense that Seth couldn't see very far from shore. He had no idea of the direction or distance to the next island. He'd have to stay put until the weather cleared.

The fog brought on the memory of another story his grandmother had told him. In it, Raven decided to get married, so he married the beautiful daughter of Chief Fog-Over-the-Salmon after promising to treat her with respect. One day his new wife sat making a basket.

'What are you making?' Raven asked her.

'You'll see,' she answered, intent on her work.

She built a large basket and filled it with seawater. Then she stirred the water with her hands. When she was done, a salmon was in the basket—the very first salmon! Raven was very happy. They cooked and ate the salmon. Thereafter, every morning she did the same thing, and they were never hungry again.

Life was good.

Eventually, though, Raven began to quarrel with his wife. It's difficult for Raven to stay nice for very long. One day he slapped her with a salmon. Because he had broken his promise to the chief, his wife ran away. Raven chased her, but every time he reached out to grab her, his hands went right through her as though she were mist. She ran into the sea, followed by every salmon she had ever made. As she waded further out into the water, she turned into the first fog.

Seth always liked that story. It seemed to explain so much, its lesson so clear. Many myths teach about the origin of things: daylight, the northern lights, mountains, or the first seal or the first salmon. Other stories, such as this one, also taught how to behave properly, with kindness, compassion, selflessness, and gratitude.

After eating a handful of berries, Seth walked along the beach and saw something that caught his attention. There was a sheen on the gently moving surface of a low-tide eddy, colorful as a swirled rainbow. He dipped his finger into the pool and studied the discoloration on his skin. He rubbed the finger against his thumb. It was slippery. He smelled it.

It was oil.

Seth knew that the great oil spill had happened nearby, but that was decades earlier. The oil mega-company had hired thousands of people to clean the beaches. But everyone knew the problem was more than skin deep. The people whose lives had been affected, mostly commercial fisherman who had lost their livelihood, sued the oil company. They won. Courts ordered the oil company to pay billions. But the giant and powerful oil company didn't pay. Instead, it kept the case in the courts for decades, always bartering down the settlement, buying time. In the ensuing years, many of the claimants—those fishermen who had lost their boats and their homes—died, and the oil company won.

The dead can't claim anything.

Curious about where the sheen was coming from, Seth used his hands to scoop away pebbles and sand from the water's edge. He dug a hole about a foot deep. His hands came up oily. The heaviest distillate of the crude oil had soaked into the soil and sands beneath the beach rocks.

It was still there.

It might always be there.

Although Seth wasn't even alive when the accident happened, he had grown up seeing the oil response sheds along the coast, each one filled with floating booms and other equipment to contain oil in event of another spill. And he had heard stories, especially from his grandmother and others, that spoke about the effects of the spill. In his grandmother's most dreadful account, the Alutiiq People who lived in the Sound were unable to hunt or fish, fearful of contamination. In fact, the government cautioned the Natives not to eat anything from land or sea.

The spill devastated the people who are of the land and of the sea.

Many of the best clam beds in the Sound were ruined.

Before the spill, herring used to swarm into the bays and coves by the billions to mate. The sea would turn milky-white from the males fertilizing the females' eggs. Afterwards, the Natives would gather the small, white egg clusters, a delicacy like *beebles*. But since the spill, the endless schools of herring hadn't returned to the region.

The more he studied the dainty, swirling oil slick, the more surprising it seemed to Seth how little it takes to destroy a thing so large as a way of life. He was unable to look away from the sheen on the sea's surface, and he felt himself holding back tears—and anger. How could he or anyone wash away all that oil with all its shimmering stain? And then it seemed to Seth that the balance of nature is precarious, a house of cards built on a ship deck in a storm.

· · · · ·

Two days later the sun evaporated the here-to-stay fog bank. As Seth awoke from a nap, he saw a ship on the horizon, it's hull as black as an oil slick. It was a tanker probably bound for Valdez, the ice-free port at the terminus of the Alaska Pipeline, which transported the crude oil all the way from the Arctic coast, eight hundred miles to the north, a monument of engineering.

Judging from its speed, Seth estimated that he had enough time to swim out far enough to attract someone's attention.

He grabbed his buoy floats and whistled to Tucker, who had been chasing seagulls down the beach. Without waiting, he plunged into the bay and swam toward the approaching ship. Tucker caught up with him, snorting from getting water in his nose. The two struck out toward the middle of the channel, passing two puffins, which quickly flew away, skimming on the surface of the water for a long time before they lifted off. Seth laughed as he watched, remembering their funny name in Alutiiq: *ngaq'ngaq*, which sounds like 'knock-knock' in a knock-knock joke.

When they were within the vessel's path, Seth waved his arms and shouted. Several times the buoys slipped from beneath his armpits, momentarily causing him to sink beneath the waves.

But the giant ship, as long as three football fields, bore down on them, unswerving, its speed never slowing. The bow seemed like a skyscraper about to fall on them. When it was apparent that the ship would neither slow nor divert its path, Seth started swimming away, back toward the island, frantically calling over his shoulder for his dog, who didn't follow but barked at the approaching menace.

'Tucker!' Seth shouted over and over, trying to catch the dog's attention.

But the sound of the tanker, now bearing down on them, was too loud. Seth started to swim back to Tucker, but he stopped after only a few strokes. There wasn't enough time to grab the dog and make it safely out of the way. They would both die in the attempt.

Reluctantly, fearing for his own life, Seth swam away.

When he was a safe distance, he turned to watch the end of his beloved and faithful friend. He watched, helplessly, as the slicing and bulbous bow of the tanker hit Tucker almost head-on. From where he was, treading in the cold sea, Seth saw the tiny speck that was his dog get heaved up into the white, frothing bow wake. Then he watched him pressed against the side of the hull for a thousand feet, sometimes going under for what seemed like too long. Seth held his breath during those times, straining to see if his dog would come up again further down the length of ship. He could only imagine what Tucker was going through: the fear, the desperation to stay afloat, to struggle to breathe as he was turned every which way, the loud hum of the passing vessel amplified whenever he went beneath the waves.

It was the stern of the tanker that most worried Seth. He had seen the propellers of tankers before, and he knew that they were as tall as a house. Tucker might survive the tumultuous dashing against the hull, but he wouldn't survive the whirling blades.

He would be chopped to pieces.

As Seth bobbed safely on the great waves of the passing ship, he watched as Tucker slid along the black hull and disappeared into the stirring aft wake.

Tucker was gone.

• • • • •

For a long time, Seth couldn't see anything but the foaming, bubbling white trail behind the propellers. But then something caught his eye several hundred yards behind the stern.

It was Tucker.

He was still alive, desperately and wearily trying to stay afloat. Seth swam toward him as fast as he could, but his progress was agonizingly slow. Twice, the dog slid below the surface, but twice he bobbed up again, like a sea otter rolling in the waves. Just before Tucker went under again, Seth reached him, wrapped both arms around his orange neck, and held his head above the water, letting the exhausted dog catch his breath, the pink buoys easily supporting them.

'Relax, boy,' he kept saying in a comforting voice. 'I've got you. You're safe now.'

Seth held Tucker for a long time, calming him, feeling his body for wounds. He seemed no worse for wear, just shaken up and slightly trembling. Eventually, the dog stopped struggling and relaxed, letting himself rest in the arms of his friend and savior. The water was colder than it had been in midsummer, and Seth was feeling its chilling effects on his muscles. While he still had enough strength, he used one arm to paddle toward shore.

He never let go of his dog with the other.

Shivering uncontrollably, Seth dragged himself and Tucker up on the beach and lay for a long time in the sun. He had learned another hard lesson.

Like the Sound, he wouldn't be saved by an oil tanker.

Qula Maquungwin

(Seventeen)

*One day, the two brothers of the young man were out hunt-
ing when they came across the carcass of their brother who
had been lost for six days. He was hanging in a tree just as
they had hung the squirrel furs at their house. They cut him
down and took his body back to the village.*

Along with darkness, autumn dragged constellations
and winter in its wake. The northern lights trailed
behind.

At first the snows were heavy and slushy, as much rain
as ice, melting shortly after falling. But eventually, as the
nights grew colder and longer, the slush turned to snow
and the whiteness stuck, like an unwelcome visitor come
to stay too long.

Now that Seth and Tucker were on the easternmost
shores of the Sound, well over a hundred miles from where

they had begun their journey, few islands remained, the distance between them too far to swim in the rapidly cooling conditions. Instead, they traveled on the mainland, the going along the coast made slow by the many meandering bays and sheer mountains that dove straight into the sea, offering uneasy passage.

But they had no choice.

One morning, before setting out for the day, Seth simply left the pink buoys on a beach. They were no longer of any use. The water was too cold to swim, they offered no shelter or warmth, and they weren't edible.

More than ever before, Seth worried about his survival.

The rubber slicker and canvas poncho were insufficient to keep them warm. Only their grueling hiking warmed them. But the nights grew more and more difficult. Even while sleeping on a thick bed of spruce boughs with the little canvas blanket covering them, Seth and Tucker shook all night long. Without fire, Seth knew that one night they would freeze to death.

Seth's tennis shoes were coming apart at the seams, and the rubber soles of both shoes were worn and loose, flapping like tongues when he walked. Seth cut two pieces of canvas from their blanket to cover his shoes, securing them around his ankles with rope. That way, he kept his feet a little drier. But the shoes weren't going to last much longer. Seth wondered how he would continue his journey without shoes, especially once the snow became impassable. The tremendous amount of approaching snowfall worried him. Back home, Seth had seen entire buildings buried under snow.

And two more things concerned him.

With little to eat, he and Tucker were losing weight much faster than before. The loss was aggravated by the fact that their bodies burned more calories simply to stay warm. Secondly, now that the silver season had ended, few boats would be plying the Sound. The chances of someone finding him fell as fast and as assuredly as the snow.

Repeatedly, with trembling hands, Seth tried to start a fire. Not once did a single spark arise from the carefully piled tinder. Without fire, it was unlikely that he and Tucker would last beyond the next couple of weeks.

It bothered Seth that he and Tucker had come so far, suffered so much, only to lose when they were so near to home. It seemed unfair. An effort such as theirs deserved reward.

But Nature doesn't think like that. To her, life is unfair and death is unfair.

As he trudged around a cove during low tide, the blanket of new-fallen snow stopping at the high tide line, Seth saw three deer foraging at the water's edge. He remembered how he and his father and Lucky sometimes went deer hunting during this time of year. They would cruise close to the beaches aboard his father's fishing boat, only a little faster than at idle, keeping a sharp eye out for deer or black bears. Upon seeing one, his father or Lucky would shut off the engine, the boat would bob in the waves, drawing no more attention than a log, and then a rifle shot would ring out across the water, its sharp report echoing in the cove. The hunters would use a dinghy or a raft to retrieve the fallen game.

Seth wished he were hunting with them now, though at the time he always resented that his father had dragged him along, tearing him away from the television, the telephone, his music, and his video games.

But he had learned something new about himself over the course of his travails, something about his sense of the world and his place in it, even though the lesson came at a high price. Like so many others, he had become disconnected from nature. He had turned his back on other people, the community of man, and even on his own heritage. He had not kept his promise to his grandmother.

As he stood on the exposed beach, looking for something to eat, he thought about his father. He wished things had been different between them. He wished he hadn't alienated himself or blamed his father after his mother's death.

If only he had taken steps to make things better. If only he had a second chance to span the sea that was forming between them. But fathers and sons rarely get such opportunities, and when they do, pride sometimes stands in the way. Pride and failed expectations: part of the history of all men.

A deep sense of regret almost blotted out his hunger.

Later that day, a violent wind arose, and the going was blocked by a steep cliff. Waves slammed against the rocky base. The water was much too dangerous and much too cold for the two of them to swim around the cliff. Instead, they would have to climb over it. After struggling to the top, Seth looked over the edge, the wind blowing his hair and beard. It was a long way down. He could see the white waves crashing against the jagged rocks below.

A terrible thought entered Seth's mind. With a single step he could end his suffering.

No more starvation. No more freezing. No more fear and loneliness.

He watched as the waves rolled in, judging the time between them, when the scraggy rocks below were most exposed.

But then he thought about Tucker, standing by his side as he had throughout their ordeal. How long would he last alone? Seth reached down and placed a hand on the dog, who looked up at him, their weary eyes holding for a long time. He couldn't do that to a friend who trusted him.

Instead, Seth cast the alluring notion over the rocky ledge.

As they climbed down the other side of the cliff, Seth felt his determination return. He hadn't given up so far, and he wasn't about to give up now, so near home, not after all he had been through. He realized he was stronger than he ever imagined.

He was still learning the expensive lesson.

The next day, the winds died and the sea calmed.

Seth was walking along the line of trees marking the edge of the beach when he heard something. He stopped moving and grabbed Tucker's collar, intent on listening. It was the sound of a boat motor, and it was very close. Seth ran to the beach just as a white boat came round a bend only about a hundred yards from the beach. It was moving slowly, only slightly faster than at idle. From where he stood, Seth could see two men on board. He ran to the very edge of the water and waved his yellow slicker, screaming at the boat.

'Here I am! Help! Over here! Over here!'

Miraculously, the bow of the boat turned landward, and to his great relief, Seth could hear the motor throttle back.

They had seen him!

Seth waded into the cold sea up to his knees, still waving his slicker.

'Over here!' he kept shouting, even though they had obviously seen him.

'Here I am!'

The calm sea rose immeasurably from his tears.

And although he couldn't read the name of the approaching boat, he saw a green shamrock painted on the side.

Seth recognized the boat.

It was the *Luck of the Irish*.

Qula Inglulen

(Eighteen)

That night, after they returned with their dead brother, a magic fog filled the village, and all the dead squirrels came back to life and returned to the Great House. Afterward, the spirit of the young man flew back into his dead body and returned him to life. From that time on, he was a great and powerful shaman who understood the connection of all living things, and The People never again killed squirrels.

W hat are you doing out here?' Joe Weil asked after helping Seth and Tucker aboard.

'I've been trying to get home,' replied Seth, his teeth chattering from his having stood in the icy water.

'You're freezing. Let's go inside and warm you up,' said the captain, leading the trembling and disheveled man and his dog into the heated galley.

Lucky brought out two blankets. He wrapped one

around Seth and the other around Tucker. He stared at the metal name tag on the dog's collar with a look of puzzlement. Finally, his eyes wide, he spoke.

'What's your name?' he asked pointedly.

Seth found it odd that Lucky would ask such a strange question. He had known him all his life.

'Lucky, it's me, Seth.'

The look of puzzlement transformed into astonishment.

'Stars! Is that really you, Seth?' he asked incredulously.

Joe Weil bent close to the rescued man's grizzled face.

'It is him!'

'But how can that be?' asked Lucky, handing Seth a cup of hot coffee. 'You've been gone for. . . .' He stopped to figure the time. 'Why, you've been missing for over four months.'

In between drinking his coffee at the small table, his trembling hands wrapped around the cup like a prayer, Seth told the story of their survival, how they had fallen overboard during the night of the storm, how they had swum from island to island, eating whatever the land or sea provided for them, raw, because they had never managed to make fire. He told them about the bears and the cave and about the tanker that almost killed Tucker.

Joe and Lucky couldn't believe how far Seth and Tucker had traveled. But their very presence was proof.

'I don't think I could have survived as long as you did,' said Lucky, shaking his head in disbelief. 'You must be starved. Let me make you something to eat.'

He quickly pan-fried two steaks, one for Seth and one for Tucker, adding some sliced potatoes and onions. It was the best meal either had eaten in their lives.

When they were done, Captain Weil called the Harbor-master on the radio.

'Come in, come in,' he said over and over, until finally someone replied on the other end.

'We found Seth Evanoff,' he said excitedly.

'Say again?' asked the Harbormaster, uncertain that he had heard correctly.

'You heard right. We found Seth Evanoff. Repeat. We found Seth. He's alive. Over. Tell his father, Seth's alive. We're bringing him home. Over.'

On the journey home, which took a little over an hour, Seth went out on deck and tossed his useless iPod into the sea, then went back inside to warm up. Lucky told him that he and Joe Weil had been deer hunting when they found him. But most important, Lucky told Seth that his father had never given up hope. He had never stopped looking for him even after everyone else had.

Seth wept at the news.

When the *Luck of the Irish* arrived in the harbor, Seth, still draped in the fluttering blanket, watched from the bow with Tucker by his side as the familiar truck pulled up and his father jumped out and raced to the end of the dock.

Moments later, Seth stood eye to eye before his father, both equally tearful. His father gripped him by the shoulders, and looked him over.

Seth was no longer the boy he had lost.

His clothes were tattered rags, his feet were wrapped in frayed canvas and bound by rope. He was an inch or two taller and much thinner—gaunt even. His father estimated that Seth had lost maybe forty or fifty pounds. His hair was long and tangled. His scraggly beard concealed most of his chiseled face, which wore a steel hardness from months of sun and wind. In his eyes was an intensity unlike anything Jack had ever seen, as deep and as wild and as sure as the sea.

Neither said a word.

For a long time, Jack Evanoff held the man his son had become, while far out in the churning Pacific, a shining multitude of salmon awaited an imperceptible signal to begin their own arduous journey home.

References

Pronunciation Glossary

The chapter numbers in this story come from the Alutiiq language of Prince William Sound, an endangered Alaska Native language. Specifically, they come from the regional dialect unique to Chenega Bay, of which the author is one of only a few surviving speakers and the editor of a dictionary. (Note: stress the capitalized syllable) See the origin of this story and the author's Alaska Native mythology books and dictionaries at www.johnsmelcer.com; click on Books and Dictionaries.

One	all'inguq	[ul-LING-ook]
Two	atel'ek	[ah-DULL-luk]
Three	pinga'an	[ping-OUN]
Four	staaman	[STAW-mun]
Five	talliman	[ta-LEE-mun]
Six	arwinlen	[ug-WAY-lin]
Seven	maquungwin	[mahk-OONG-win]
Eight	inglulen	[ing-LOO-lin]
Nine	qulnguan	[kool-NEW-yen]
Ten	qulen	[koo-LEN]
Eleven	qula all'inguq	[koo-la ul-LING-ook]
Twelve	qula atel'ek	[koo-la ah-DULL-luk]

Thirteen	qula pinga'an	[koo-la ping-OUN]
Fourteen	qula staaman	[koo-la STAW-mun]
Fifteen	qula talliman	[koo-la ta-LEE-mun]
Sixteen	qula arwinlen	[koo-la ug-WAY-lin]
Seventeen	qula maquungwin	[koo-la mahk-OONG-win]
Eighteen	qula inglulen	[koo-la ing-LOO-lin]

The Author

John Smelcer is the poetry editor of *Rosebud* magazine and the author of more than forty books, including 2013's *Lone Wolves* (Leapfrog Press). He is an enrolled member of the Ahtna tribe and is now the last tribal member who reads and writes in Ahtna. John holds degrees in anthropology and archaeology, linguistics, literature, and education. He also holds a PhD in English and creative writing from Binghamton University, and formerly chaired the Alaska Native Studies program at the University of Alaska Anchorage.

His first novel, *The Trap*, was an American Library Association BBYA Top Ten Pick, a VOYA Top Shelf Selection, and a New York Public Library Notable Book. *The Great Death* was short-listed for the 2011 William Allen White Award, and nominated for the National Book Award, the BookTrust Prize (England), and the American Library Association's Award for American Indian YA Literature. His

Alaska Native mythology books include *The Raven and the Totem* (introduced by Joseph Campbell). His short stories, poems, essays, and interviews have appeared in hundreds of magazines, and he is the winner of the 2004 Milt Kessler Poetry Book Award and of the 2004 Western Writers of America Award for Poetry for his collection *Without Reservation*, which was nominated for a Pulitzer. John divides his time between a cabin in Talkeetna, the climbing capitol of Alaska, and Kirksville, Mo., where he is a visiting scholar in the Department of Communications Studies at Truman State University.

The Illustrator

Hannah Carlon, 17, lives in the village of Centerville, Mass., on Cape Cod. She has studied with fine arts teacher Eiblis Cazealt, painter Carl Lopes, and mixed media painter/figure drawing artist Sarah Holl. In 2014, she showcased her art in the Massachusetts State House, the Heritage Museum and Gardens, and the Barnstable Town Hall. She will be attending Lesley University in September 2014 to study art therapy.

Discussion Questions & Activities

1. Describe Seth physically and emotionally at the *beginning* of the novel. What are some of his habits? Can you see yourself in Seth? Describe Seth physically and emotionally at the *end* of the novel. How has he changed both outside and inside?

2. Why are Seth and his father estranged? Do you think their relationship will change?

3. Seth's Native heritage played an important role in his survival. Is there anything you have learned from your heritage that might help you survive in the wilderness? Do you think you are self-sufficient enough to survive in the wilderness the way Seth did?

4. Discuss the scene where Seth's father goes into the local bar to ask other fisherman for help. He's lost his wife and now he thinks he may have lost his son as well. What do you think he must be feeling? Have you ever lost someone close to you? How did it make you feel?

5. What's Tucker's role in the story? Seth lost a lot of weight during his ordeal, but he always shared his food with Tucker. He could have just kept it for himself. Why did he risk his own well-being for a dog?

6. How did Seth's isolation help him through the grieving process? Could the same be true for his father?

7. The cave with the skeletons of Japanese soldiers from WWII really exists. As a project, research The Aleutian War in WWII and learn more about the Japanese invasion of Alaska's Aleutian Islands. How did this impact the people who lived on those islands?

8. Seth was never able to build a fire. As a class project, arrange to go outside and try to start a campfire using only what nature provides: sticks, rocks, grass, moss, twigs. Despite what we see in the movies, is it easy to start a fire without matches or a lighter?

9. Seth goes without technology for several months—no texting, music, videos, video games, or social media. The average high school student today texts 3,000 times a month. Would you give that up for just one week? Discuss how digital technology impacts your life and how much of it you could do without.

Lone Wolves
John Smelcer

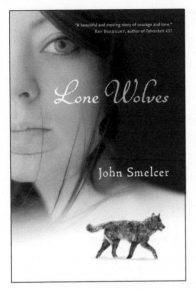

Deneena Yazzie isn't like other 16-year-old girls in her village. Her love of the woods and trail come from her grandfather, who teaches her the all-but-vanished Native Alaskan language and customs. While her peers lose hope, trapped between the old and the modern cultures, Denny and her mysterious lead dog, a blue-eyed wolf, train for the Great Race—a thousand-mile test of courage and endurance through the vast Alaskan wilderness. Denny learns the value of intergenerational friendships, of maintaining connections to her heritage, and of being true to herself, and in her strength she gives her village a new pride and hope.

"A beautiful and moving story of courage and love."—Ray Bradbury

"With this inspiring young adult novel, Smelcer promises to further solidify his status as "Alaska's modern-day Jack London.'"—*Mushing* magazine, Suzanne Steinert

"Powerful, eloquent, and fascinating, showcasing a vanishing way of life in rich detail."—*Kirkus*

"An engaging tale of survival, love, and courage."—*School Library Journal*

Savage Mountain
John Smelcer

(Leapfrog Press – Summer 2015)

Summer, 1980. Brothers Sebastian and James Savage decide to climb one of the highest mountains in Alaska to prove themselves to their father, whose respect they can never seem to earn. Inspired by true events, *Savage Mountain* is not a story of father-son reconciliation. Some relationships can never be mended. Instead, it's a touching story of two brothers who test their limits and learn that the way their father treats them is not their fault, and no matter how different they might be from each other, the strongest bond of all is brotherhood.

"Smelcer clearly knows his way around Alaskan mountains."
—David Roberts, author of *The Mountain of My Fear, True Summit, Deborah,* and *The Lost Explorer: Finding Mallory on Mt. Everest*